AVENGING CHRISTA

IRRESISTIBLY MINE DUET BOOK 2

TRACIE DELANEY

M. A. COMLEY

BOOKS BY TRACIE DELANEY

The Winning Ace Series

Cash - A Winning Ace Short Story

Winning Ace

Losing Game

Grand Slam

Winning Ace Boxset

Mismatch

Break Point - A Winning Ace Novella

Stand-alone

My Gift To You

The Brook Brothers Series

The Blame Game

Against All Odds

His To Protect

Web of Lies

Irresistibly Mine Series

Tempting Christa

Avenging Christa

For Mel - simply the best

1

DAYTON

"I love you, Dayton. But I love Max more. I'm sorry."

Christa's words tore through me. As swiftly as wet fingers snuffing out a candle, my world imploded. She didn't mean it, *couldn't* mean it. After everything we'd been through, all we'd overcome, the *family* we'd built...

Atwood could go fuck himself. I would not allow that psychopath to ruin the best thing that had ever happened to me. Christa, Max, and me, we were a team—and God help anyone who tried to tear us apart.

I watched the love of my life, my heart, my soul, my... my *everything*, clutching her son, her arms wrapped tightly around him. She kissed the top of his head, her eyes on me, waiting for my reaction. No, not waiting.

Fearing.

Oh God, no. I was as bad as *him*. This was all my fault. My inability to rein it in, to show some restraint, had brought us to this point. And now I'd have to live with the consequences.

"Angel, please listen to me. I hear what you're saying, but I won't let you fight this alone. I'll do whatever it takes. Please don't give up on me. On us. I will *never* allow that fu—Atwood to take Max."

Her watery gaze met mine. "It's in the hands of the courts now. You can't stop him. No one can."

"Momma, down," Max demanded, wriggling in Christa's arms, thankfully, completely oblivious to the war about to be waged with him right in the middle of it.

Christa set him down on the floor, and he waddled off to go play with his toys. Christ, the innocence… There were no limits, no lengths I wouldn't go to, when it came to protecting him and Christa.

In desperation, I clutched her upper arms. "We can stop him, providing we stick together. If you let him push us apart, then that'll weaken your chances. Trust me, please. I will fix this."

"How?" she asked, her voice hoarse, raw, broken. "How will you fix it?"

I had no freaking clue—yet—but problem-solving was in my blood, a skill I used every day in my work life. This wouldn't be any different. In fact, I'd relish the chance to ruin that bastard.

"Do you trust me?" I asked, purposely ignoring her question.

"Yes."

Her instantaneous response sparked a flicker of hope that maybe she hadn't given up on me just yet.

I caressed her face, memorizing every inch in case there was ever a time when I needed to recall how her skin felt beneath my fingers. I brushed my lips tenderly over hers, the spark of hope turning into a flame when she kissed me back.

"I won't let you down," I whispered. "Give me a chance to prove I'm worthy of your trust."

Her bottom lip wobbled. "I'm scared, Dayton. I can't lose my baby, especially not to him."

"Max is going nowhere," I reiterated. "We'll play Atwood's games, go along with his petition, but I want you to know that I'll be working in the background to make this right." I took a breath. She wasn't going to like what I had to say. "Prepare yourself, angel, because the judge will likely award visitation rights automatically while the rest of the custody hearing takes place."

She paled and shoved a trembling hand through her hair. "You're right. Of course you're right. Why wouldn't they give him access? In the eyes of the law, he's an innocent man." Tears spilled down her cheeks. "I can't do this."

My heart squeezed with agony while my spine stiffened with rage. That bastard would suffer, not only for what he had done to Christa in the past, but also for what he was trying to do to her now. My nostrils flared, my hands subconsciously curled into fists. I caught Christa's wide-eyed stare and quickly unfurled them, stuffing them into my pockets. The last thing she needed was to be reminded of what lurked beneath the surface, of how much anger I held within me, of my ability to unleash it on anyone who hurt the people I loved the most. Violence was her trigger, her red flag, the very thing that hauled her back to what *he'd* done, the depravity of *his* revenge. I inhaled, releasing the breath slowly, calming my inner demons. Christa didn't need my fury. She needed my support.

I might not have figured out how I could drive Atwood from our lives for good, but I knew how to be patient when the situation called for it. I was well versed in being dogged, determined, single-minded. Just ask my father.

I wrapped my arms around her and kissed the top of her head. "We'll handle him together. I'm with you every step of the way. You're not alone in this."

———

"That's not good enough."

Eric, my Head of Legal, and one of the most ferocious commercial counsels in the country, sighed heavily down the phone. "Dayton, be reasonable. Family law isn't my thing. I need to make some calls. What difference is twenty-four hours going to make?"

To Christa's sanity? A whole fucking lot.

"You've got twelve, Eric. Make them count."

I hung up. Wearily, I swept a hand over my face. The atmosphere in the car on the drive back to Manhattan had been tighter than an archer's bow with Christa retreating inside herself, nibbling on her fingernails and staring out the window, causing a huge knot of anxiety to grow in my stomach. One that was still there, gnawing away at me.

I wandered back into the living room, ordered some food, and poured us each a glass of wine while I waited for her to appear. She did, ten minutes later, her face bruised with exhaustion, her shoulders drooped, her skin pale. I beckoned to her, and she sat beside me then rested her head on my shoulder.

"Max okay?"

Her head bobbed. "Out like a light."

"I've ordered Chinese food."

"I'm not hungry."

"Neither am I, but try to eat something, for me."

She straightened and picked up her drink, taking a larger than normal swig. "I needed that."

I tucked her hair behind her ear. "I called my Head of Legal. He's going to source a couple of names of excellent family lawyers. I'm going to make an appointment for Monday."

She stared into space, her fingertip absentmindedly circling the rim of her glass. "How did it come to this?" She shook her head, meeting my worried gaze. "I'm so sorry, Dayton. I didn't mean to bring all this trouble to your door."

"Hey now." I removed the glass from her hand and set it on the table, then nestled her into my side once more. "You, me, and Max. We're a family. You've both brought such joy to my life, Christa. This is merely a bump in the road." *And one I'm going to obliterate.*

She snorted. "Understatement of the century."

I grinned. "What can I say? I'm a winner."

She laughed, the first time in what felt like days, but all too soon, her face fell. "You don't know what he's like. He doesn't care about Max. He only cares about hurting me. He won't stop until I've paid the debt he thinks I owe him." Her voice broke, and she wrung her hands. "He wants retribution, and he knows that choosing to go after Max will hurt me the most."

"He won't get custody of Max."

She shook her head forcefully. "He could, Dayton." She grabbed a cushion and hugged it to her belly, then tossed it to one side, gripping her hair instead. "God, he might. I have to face facts, because if I don't prepare myself and the worst happens..." She scrubbed her face, then let her hands flop into her lap. "I know you're trying to shield me, but it's honesty that will make me strong, not well-meant half-truths. Sutton could win custody of Max. At the very least, shared custody."

A burst of anger erupted within me. "Over my dead body."

I launched to my feet. Christa silently watched as I prowled around the room like a caged animal, my hands clenched into fists. What I wouldn't give to punch Atwood's face, beating him until he begged me for mercy, all the while knowing that by acting out on the fantasy, I could be the reason Christa lost Max. No, if I was to win the war against Atwood, I'd need to be cunning, and have patience, not rage.

After a few seconds of watching me stomp around, Christa shot to her feet. She stood in front of me, hands planted on her hips. "Dayton, calm the hell down. I know you're trying to protect me, to protect Max, but lying to me, and to yourself, about what we're facing won't do either of us any good." She pinched the bridge of her nose and closed her eyes for a brief second. "Don't treat me like a child. Treat me like your equal. Don't you see? Our power is in our love for each other, and for Max. It's what will drive us forward, keep us going when shit gets rough. Because it will, and it's going to be awful, just awful. Only by sticking together, by being *completely* honest with each other will we get through this."

As I gazed at her, my chest burst with pride. She was in the middle of a nightmare, terrified of losing her son, and her own sanity in the process, and yet still she responded with dignity, with reasonable, rational thought. Once she'd recovered from the initial shock of Atwood's release, she'd grown a spine of steel.

"You really are an amazing woman."

She gave me a faint smile, then tucked herself into my arms. "Max gives me strength, but it's your faith and belief in me, your support and your love, that will ultimately give me the power to beat him." She tilted her head back, a determined glint in her eyes. "And I will."

2

CHRISTA

My heels clicked on the marble floor, the sound echoing down the hallway. I leaned forward, walking more on the balls of my feet to minimize the noise. Nerves filled my stomach, and my palms felt unpleasantly clammy. Francesca Hale, one of the most sought-after family lawyers on the east coast, had agreed to take my case. *Mine.* Talk about surreal. I had Dayton to thank, though. If it had been me on my own, I'd have had no chance of securing her services.

We took a seat outside Francesca's office. Pressing my knees together, I rested my hands in my lap, tapping my fingers on the top of my thighs. My priority was preventing Sutton from gaining any sort of permanent custody to Max. I'd already acknowledged that he'd be given temporary access. I didn't need a lawyer to tell me we'd lose that concession. From a legal standpoint, the courts would see Sutton as an upstanding member of the Seattle community, a rich, successful businessman who exuded charm and sophistication.

I knew different. I'd seen what the monster behind the mask was capable of. Every time I allowed my mind to wander, to think about handing over Max to him, panic simmered to the surface. No, I couldn't go there.

One baby step at a time. That was how I'd chosen to deal with this. Bite-size chunks.

Dayton squeezed my hand. I offered up a wavering smile, which was all I could manage. Without him and his unfailing support, not to mention his deep pockets, I'd have had no chance of beating Sutton. Without Dayton in my corner, the probability of losing my son would be much greater.

"You can go in now."

I acknowledged Francesca's assistant with a succinct nod and rose from my chair. I slipped my hand inside Dayton's, straightened my spine, and took a deep breath.

That's it, Christa. Professional and in control on the outside. And a complete mess on the inside.

Francesca Hale wasn't at all like I expected. I'd seen her photograph on her website, but she was much younger in person, and tall—only an inch or two shorter than Dayton—with long, straight blonde hair and the kind of eyes that saw everything. Keen, almost hawk-like. I immediately took to her.

She stood as we entered, then rounded her desk to greet us. "Mr. Somers, Ms. Adams, lovely to meet you." We shook hands, and she gestured to the two chairs opposite her desk. "Please, have a seat."

"Thank you for seeing us at such short notice," Dayton said as I tucked my skirt beneath me and sat.

Francesca picked up her pen and hovered the tip over a yellow legal pad. "Eric gave me some scant details, but why don't you start from the beginning."

Dayton looked over at me, and I began talking. Once I started, I couldn't stop, apart from the odd time to take a sip of water to quench my parched throat. Having laid out the details as objectively as I could, I sucked in a calming breath while ignoring the chill creeping over my skin and continued.

"Sutton wants to make me pay. He blames me for putting him in jail, and now he's back to demand his pound of flesh. He isn't doing this because he wants Max. He only wants to hurt me, to make me suffer, and he knows the best way to do that is through my son."

I wiped my sweaty palms on my skirt and swallowed. Dayton touched my elbow.

"Are you okay?"

I nodded, biting my lip.

Francesca set her pen down. Her neat handwriting had filled several sheets of paper. I idly wondered why she didn't use a tablet or a laptop. My hand would ache if I wrote that many pages.

She linked her fingers and met my gaze. "Thank you for being so honest and articulate. You've made my job a lot easier. You'd be surprised the number of clients who leave out bits and pieces where they think the information might show them in a bad light." She turned her attention to Dayton then back to me. "Okay, so here's what we're going to do. Absolutely nothing."

My eyes widened, and my lips parted. "Nothing?"

She nodded. "Correct. Let him make the first move. He has to file a motion with the court first before we can counter, so let him get on with that. In the meantime, here's my advice. We hire a private detective to find out everything we can about this guy. And I mean everything. We dig hard and deep into his background, his past, from childhood to now. No one is off the table. Ex-girlfriends, ex-employees, disgruntled family members. Any one of them might have information to share that will help your case if and when he does file for custody. We use the time we have now to our advantage, because once the courts get going, we're in the system and we'll have to run to their timescales." Her pen rolled to the side, and she picked it up, then fixed her attention directly on Dayton. "I hope you're heavily invested in winning, Mr. Somers, because this is going to get expensive real fast. Good private investigators can run into the tens of thousands."

Tens of thousands?

I gulped. "Dayton—"

"Money doesn't come into this," he said, cutting me off. "What matters is Christa and Max." He clutched my fingers and squeezed. "In terms of a private investigator, I'm happy to interview whoever you recommend, but I will also be reaching out to my own contacts."

Francesca frowned. "That's not how this usually works, Mr. Somers. I have tried and tested private investigators who I work with on cases such as these."

"I don't care. I'm not saying I don't trust you. I'm saying I don't trust anyone." He picked a piece of lint off his dark trousers. "This is going to get dirty. An element of plausible deniability for you wouldn't be a bad thing. Better that you stay squeaky clean and let me bury my hands in the filth. Regardless of how you reconcile this, Ms. Hale, I will be selecting my own team." He fell silent, his gaze locked on Francesca's.

My heart drummed against my ribcage as Dayton and Francesca stared each other down. Francesca, despite being as hard-boiled as they come, was the first to blink. She turned her gaze to the window and rubbed her middle finger over her lips, considering. Eventually, her focus returned to Dayton. "It's highly irregular, but okay, Mr. Somers, we'll try this your way. However, I will need to be kept fully informed."

Dayton nodded. "Of course."

Francesca tapped the pen on her pad. "Have they released the actual perpetrator of the crime, too?" she asked, refocusing on me. "The man who carried out the assault?"

I shook my head. "I don't think so. I'm not sure, to be honest. The DA's office in Seattle haven't exactly been forthcoming with information. They didn't even call me to let me know Sutton had been released."

"I'll find out. I doubt they have, but I prefer facts to conjecture. I'll put him down as a person of interest. I might want to talk to him, depending on how things progress. That is, of course, if Mr. Atwood carries through with his threat."

"He will," I said firmly, because it was true. Sutton didn't make idle threats. I knew that better than most.

Francesca gave me a reassuring smile. "Try not to worry. I know that sounds trite, and likely impossible for you, but until he actually files a motion, there isn't much more we can do other than what we've discussed." Her lips pressed into a thin line, giving me the impression that she still wasn't happy with Dayton and how he wanted to run things.

I stood, nodded, and shook her hand once more. Dayton followed suit.

"We'll be in touch." Dayton pressed his hand into the small of my back and guided me outside. "She's good," he said as we exited the elevator into the lobby.

"And expensive," I said with a grimace. "I mean her fees, and the private investigator…" I blew out a slow breath. "Tens of thousands she said."

Dayton wrapped his arm around my waist. "Christa, stop worrying." His voice held a tinge of weariness. I wasn't sure whether that was because of me, or our situation, or both. "It's nothing."

"To you," I said. "To me, it's a fortune. I don't like spending your money, Dayton. It isn't right."

His cheeks puffed up as he blew out a breath. Drawing to a halt, he forced me to stop alongside him. He caught my hips and tugged me closer, then tipped up my chin until I met his gaze. "I don't want to hear it. You're my girlfriend, my lover, my life. Hell, we live together. What's mine is yours."

I opened my mouth to speak until he stopped me with a look. The kind of expression I'd learned not to argue with.

"This is the last time we're having this conversation. Money for the sake of it is meaningless. Spending it to secure your happiness and Max's rightful place in the center of our family is precisely what I worked for all these years, even if I wasn't aware of it at the time. I don't care if this case costs tens of millions. It's loose change. I'd give my last cent to wipe Sutton Atwood from your life once and for all. Hiring a top lawyer to help us fight our corner is just good business. Now please drop it."

He grabbed my hand and strode outside without giving me a chance to respond. I trotted beside him, my tail firmly between my legs, but with a lightness in my heart. For the first time, I dared to believe we might just have a chance of winning.

3

DAYTON

I WALKED into the bar and scanned around. No sign of Cole yet. I'd first met Detective Brook two years ago after an attempted break-in at my penthouse. My sister, Nina, had been visiting and was home alone. She'd been shaken but not hurt, and the thieves had escaped with nothing. The detective had given me some great advice on security upgrades, and our paths had crossed a few times since then. I liked the guy. He had a sharp eye for detail, and I trusted him about as much as I trusted anyone. I was hoping Cole could introduce me to a couple of private detectives. I'd already spoken to the guy Francesca had recommended.

Let's just say that we didn't hit it off.

"Dayton, sorry I'm late." Cole clapped me on the shoulder then slipped into the seat opposite. "Long time no see."

"I only just got here myself. Thanks for meeting with me." I invited over the server. "Drink?"

"A beer would be good."

"Two beers," I said.

"Coming right up." The server ventured behind the bar to fetch our drinks, returning a minute later.

We shared pleasantries until she moved on to the next customer.

"What can I do for you?" Cole asked. "You sounded a little cryptic on the phone."

"I need a private investigator," I said. "A top-notch one. Someone discreet. Money is no object. I'm interested in the kind of individual who'll dig deep and go hard. I want every secret found, every stone overturned, every corner explored."

"May I ask who for?" He held up his hands. "Not that it's any of my business. Color me curious."

I threaded my fingers together and rested my hands on the table. "My girlfriend's ex."

Cole's eyebrows shot up. "Sounds interesting."

Until that moment, I hadn't made up my mind exactly how much to share, but sitting there with Cole, I had an urge to offload the whole sorry mess. After all, what Christa had gone through was a matter of public record. It wasn't as though I'd be breaking her confidence by telling Cole, and if I shared everything, hopefully he'd take me seriously and recommend the big guns. I didn't want some two-bit private eye who made their living spying on cheating husbands.

"We might need a few more beers. It's a long story."

Cole removed his phone from his inside pocket. "I'll text Millie and let her know I'll be late." He tapped on the screen then put his phone away. "She's due in seven weeks, so I don't like her to worry."

"Looking forward to baby number two?"

Cole grinned. "Can't wait. You should try it sometime."

"My girlfriend has a son. He'll be three in September."

"They're great at that age, aren't they? Aimee's almost four now, and there isn't a day that goes by she doesn't bring us joy."

I smiled. I never thought I'd like being around kids. Turned out I was wrong. Maybe one day, when our current challenge was dealt with, we might even have one of our own. Wrong time for thoughts along those lines, though. Until this shit with Atwood was behind us, we had no chance of moving forward with our lives.

"Sorry," Cole said. "I went off on a tangent. Fill me in."

By the time I'd finished, Cole's expression had changed from warm and open to cold and hardened, his jaw clenched tight, his eyes glistening with barely contained fury.

"What a bastard."

I nodded. "Christa is worried sick he'll get custody, and although I try to say all the right things to her, between us, I'm concerned. Atwood will definitely use the beating I gave Arek Kawalski against me—he already told Christa that—and because Atwood's conviction has been rescinded, we can't use that information as part of our reasoning why he shouldn't be allowed anywhere near Max."

"Hence the PI to hopefully dig up enough dirt to bury the fucker."

"Precisely."

Cole rubbed his chin. "I don't know anyone in Seattle, or even the west coast. All my contacts are here. However, my ex-partner recently moved into the private investigation and personal security field. High-end type clients. He may have better luck recommending someone, or at least be able to give you more advice. If you're willing for me to share, I can give him a call."

"Is he trustworthy?"

Cole laughed. "I'd trust him with my life."

I gestured to him. "Then let's give him a call."

After he phoned his former partner, and I listened to their banter, the closeness between them evident. A couple of minutes later, he hung up.

"He's not very far away. If you can hang around, he's heading over to meet us."

We ordered another round of beers, as well as one for Cole's friend. When he arrived, my mouth dropped open. I hadn't expected *that*. The guy who clapped Cole hard enough to dislocate his shoulder was nothing short of a giant. I was over six feet —same as Cole—but this guy must have been at least six inches taller than us, broad in the chest, with long hair, a straggly beard, and tattoos that covered his arms and hands.

"Shift over, dickhead," he growled, sliding into the seat next to Cole.

He held out a hand, which I shook. I tried not to wince. The guy had a hell of a grip.

"I'm Draven," he said. "You must be Dayton." He boomed out a laugh that caused several people at nearby tables to crane their necks before quickly averting their gazes. "That could get confusing."

"We could always use your first name," Cole said, grinning. "No confusion then."

Draven glowered. "We could. Of course, I'd rip out your tongue before you uttered a single syllable."

Cole laughed, clearly not the least concerned by the threat. He pressed his palm to his chest. "I'll take it to my grave."

"Which you'll be inhabiting earlier than you anticipated if you mention that shit again."

More laughter from Cole. I guessed Draven wasn't all that fond of his first name. As they bantered back and forth, I sat there, slightly envious of their bond. I had a lot of acquaintances but no real close male friends. I'd lost touch with everyone from school after my father threw me out on my sixteenth birthday, and ever since then all my energies had gone into creating, and then growing, my business. I had no time to form the kind of friendship these two shared.

I had Christa, though. And Max. A real family, something I'd assumed was for other people rather than myself. My life had taken a different turn from Cole and Draven, that was all.

"Anyway, down to business," Draven said. "Unlike this

cock"—he jerked his head in Cole's direction—"I have a real job. Cole mentioned you needed a PI."

I nodded. "The best. And I need them quick."

"The best and readily available don't usually go together. Good people are in high demand."

"I'm aware of that," I said, bristling. "I run a multi-billion-dollar company."

Draven quirked an eyebrow. "Easy, brother. Just stating facts."

"The facts are that my girlfriend could very well lose her son to a complete psychopath unless I do something to stop him. All I'm asking for is a name, a recommendation. I'll do the negotiating from there."

Draven's eyebrow rose farther. "You could always kill him. That'd stop him."

Cole clamped his hands over his ears. "For fuck's sake, Draven. You might not work at the NYPD any longer, but I fucking do."

A smile inched across my face. These two were fantastic. "Not really my style," I said, smoothing a hand over my shirt. "I'm not averse to walking the line, though. Those kinds of shenanigans go on in board rooms all over the country every day."

Draven shrugged. "Fair enough." He stroked his beard. "I might know the right individual for the job. I'll need a couple of days to set it up."

"How about I give you until tomorrow. I'm on a clock."

Draven's lips twitched, and he held out his hand, palm up. "Gimme your contact details."

I gave him my business card. He gave it a cursory glance then slid it into the front pocket of his leather jacket. He lifted his beer bottle, clinked it against Cole's, then took a long swig. When his eyes met mine again, they flickered with interest.

"So, tell me more about this fucking lunatic."

4

CHRISTA

"CHRISTA."

Dayton's soothing voice came at me through a sleepy haze. I groaned, then turned over, burrowing underneath the covers. I had no idea what time it was, but as I'd lain awake half the night worrying, finally drifting off as dawn broke, I desperately needed more sleep. My eyelids refused to open.

"Christa." He tugged at the comforter. "I have to go into the office."

That got my attention. We still had a day of our interrupted vacation left, plus the upcoming weekend when Dayton had promised we'd take Max to the zoo. I rolled onto my back and squinted at him through one eye. The other one stubbornly remained closed. He was already dressed in a dark-gray suit with a matching striped tie and a crisp white shirt. My breath caught at the sight of him in his business attire. Suits were made for men like Dayton.

"Why?" I asked, my voice drowsy with sleep. "You look damned sexy by the way."

He chuckled and tugged at a stray hair that had caught the

corner of my mouth, then brushed his lips over mine. "Nothing for you to worry about. I should be home early this afternoon."

I stretched my arms overhead and yawned. "I don't want you to go."

"Neither do I, especially with you thrusting your chest out like that."

I grasped his tie, letting the silk feed through my fingers, and pulled him closer. "You smell good, too." I buried my nose in his neck and breathed deeply. "Do you have to go right now?"

His breath hitched, and he bent down to kiss me again, this time deeper. He slid his tongue over my bottom lip, and I opened my mouth to welcome him in. We kissed, passionately, the kind that sent tingles to my fingers and toes. I wanted it to go on forever, but too soon, he drew back.

"You're irresistible, you know that? You're definitely not making things easy for me, but look at it this way: the sooner I go, the sooner I'll be back, and then..." He left the sentence lingering, his words full of promise.

"I'm holding you to that," I said, stretching again, the movement drawing a low groan from Dayton.

"Christa, you're killing me."

I grinned. "What time is it?"

"Six-thirty."

I rubbed my eyes. "I don't think I fell asleep until four."

His teasing expression fell. "Christa…"

"I know. I know. There's nothing to be done until Sutton makes a move. I think that's half the problem. The waiting."

"In the knowledge that my pleas will fall on deaf ears, please try not to worry." He glanced at his watch. "I really do need to go, but I hate leaving you like this."

"Go, go." I shooed him away. "I'll be fine. Max and I will get some fresh air or something."

His mouth turned down at the edges, and I inwardly kicked

myself for burdening him unnecessarily. He grazed his knuckles down my cheek. "Love you."

My heart squeezed. I curved a hand around the back of his neck and raised myself for a final goodbye kiss. "I love you."

After Dayton left, I fetched Max and settled him in front of the TV with his morning milk. I fixed us some breakfast, yet as I cleared away, dark thoughts crowded in. I was terrified of losing Dayton, but if it came down to a choice between him and Max… well, there was no choice. If the courts showed any concern about Max being around Dayton, I'd have to move out, end our relationship. *I* knew Max was completely safe, that Dayton would never hurt either of us, but the courts only went on facts, and those facts were that Dayton had a temper, even if his anger only surfaced when he felt the need to protect those he loved. Dayton might be loving and adoring to us, but he rarely let the outside world see that side of him. The legal system didn't understand how kind, generous, and caring he was. They'd simply look at the evidence, and my concern was that, on paper, Dayton wouldn't come off well.

Max giggled at something on the TV, dragging my attention back to the present. The penthouse was so eerie without Dayton. Despite the large open-plan space, the walls seemed to close in. I needed to get out, to grab some fresh air, take a walk, get some exercise. As I put my cup in the sink, my gaze fell on a flyer I'd been handed before we'd gone on vacation. It was for a local parenting group. At the time I hadn't paid it much attention, especially as I worked full time and spent my weekends with Dayton, but now, rattling around this overly big home with nothing to occupy my racing mind, it seemed like the ideal solution. Somewhere to pass the time for a few hours, talking to other moms with kids Max's age.

With renewed focus, I checked their opening times then strapped Max into his stroller and set off. Half an hour later, I arrived at the right address. It reminded me of the childcare facility at Dayton's company with lots of toys strewn around and excitable kids having fun. Unsure what to do, I hovered around the entrance until Joanna, the woman who ran it, welcomed me. Soon, I was sitting with the other moms drinking coffee and chatting about our kids.

But, despite my best efforts, I found myself only half joining in. I watched Max sitting in the middle of the floor, playing with the other children. My chest tightened. Right there was my reason for living. I would always put him first. Always. A lump formed in my throat, and I swallowed. Why was life so unfair? Why might *I* be forced to choose Max over Dayton? I wanted them both, but Sutton could very well make that impossible should he follow through with his threat to show Dayton as unfit to be around Max, and the courts found in Sutton's favor.

My eyes prickled, and I blinked to clear my vision. I put down my cup a little too heavily, drawing the attention of Joanna who was sitting across from me.

"Christa, are you okay?"

I nodded, scrambling to my feet. I managed to croak out, "Sorry, I just remembered I need to be somewhere." Striding over to the play area, I picked up Max, who bawled as I put him in his stroller, clearly furious at my decision to cut short his fun. I caught the surprised looks on the moms' faces as I hurriedly left.

I hadn't walked far when a prickling sensation crept up my spine. I paused, my hands tight on the stroller, then swung around ready to confront the reason for my unease. The streets teemed with people going about their business, but as I scanned the crowds, nothing struck me as out of the ordinary. Still, I quickened my steps, even crossing the street in an attempt to shake off the edginess coursing through me. My palms were slick with sweat by the time my building came into view. The second I stepped into the lobby, I let out a relieved breath, chastising myself for being so paranoid.

I crossed to our private elevator and jabbed my finger at the button, knowing that as soon as I was inside the car, my anxiety would recede. Out of the corner of my eye, I spotted a man approaching from my left. I didn't know everyone in Dayton's building—far from it—but something about this guy set my teeth on edge. I fumbled in my purse for my phone, wishing I had a can of Mace, or a bunch of keys, something with which I could protect myself. The security guard was a little too far away for my liking if this guy had harm on his mind.

"Ms. Adams? Ms. Christa Adams?" he asked.

I stood protectively in front of Max's stroller. "Yes." The high-pitched squeak to my voice gave me away. I cleared my throat. "Who wants to know?"

He thrust an envelope at me.

"What's this?"

"Court papers, ma'am."

Oh God. This was it. I'd been served. Sutton had made his move. The moment I'd dreaded since he'd called a few days earlier had arrived. I stared at the envelope for a few seconds, and by the time I lifted my chin, the guy was already halfway out of the building, whistling as he went.

The elevator doors opened and, on shaky legs, I pushed Max inside. The second we entered the penthouse, he demanded his lunch. As I prepared food for Max, my gaze wandered to the stack of papers sitting on the coffee table, daring me to open them. Except I didn't want to. Reading the contents of that inconspicuous brown envelope would force me to face reality, to acknowledge this was really happening.

I thought I'd hated Sutton before, but that was nothing to how I felt about him now. Using my son to punish me was beyond heinous and, no matter what the legal outcome, I'd find a way to make him pay—even if it took me the rest of my life.

I settled Max in front of the TV with a sandwich and picked up the envelope. I stared at it for a few seconds, then turned it over. I slid a fingernail underneath the flap and removed a wad of documents. They were full of official jargon, but I didn't need to be a legal expert to recognize that Sutton was applying for immediate visitation rights, as well as full custody of Max on the basis he was living in a violent home. I wasn't the least bit surprised Sutton had carried out his promise. He wasn't the type to throw around idle threats—rather he was the following-through kind of psychopath.

My stomach swirled and churned. The fight I'd dreaded was at my door, and I only had a few days to prepare. I might not win every battle along the way… but I'd damn well win the war.

5

DAYTON

MY DRIVER, Paul, dropped me right outside my office building. As I entered the lobby, the man I'd come to meet rose to greet me.

"Draven. Good to see you again." We shook hands. "Your message caught me off guard. I thought you were going to recommend someone."

"You said you wanted the best." He threw his arms out to the side and grinned. "I am the best."

"Confidence? I like it. I can definitely get on board with that." I cocked my head. "Follow me."

I strode over to my private elevator which took us directly to my office. Angie wasn't at her desk yet, not that I expected her to be in this early. Even I wasn't that demanding.

I opened the door and ushered Draven inside. "Coffee?" I asked.

He held up his hand. "I'm good."

I took a seat at the head of the conference table and gestured to the one adjacent. I'd stayed up late the previous night preparing a briefing note on everything I knew about Atwood. His name, a picture, his business address, all stuff that I'd gleaned from his company website, but at least it meant Draven didn't have to take notes. I handed over the sheet of paper.

"This is the guy I told you about. I want you to find out everything about him. Go back to the day he was fucking born if you have to, but somewhere in his past there's dirt. I want to know what that is."

I knew how powerful men worked. We all had skeletons in our closets that we'd rather weren't released into the public domain. Mine was my abused background. I didn't choose to hide what my father did to Nina and me because I was ashamed —I wasn't—but because some would see it as a weakness and use it to try to exploit me.

All I needed was to find Atwood's Achilles heel, and the guy sitting beside me was going to help me do precisely that.

Draven scanned the sheet of paper then folded it and slid it into his inside pocket. "My rates are fifteen hundred per day plus expenses."

"Fine."

"I'll need a week up front. Cash if possible."

I rose from my chair, went across to the safe, and withdrew several stacks of bills. I handed them to Draven. "I want a daily report, more often than that if you find something of interest. You have my contact details. I can be reached any time, day or night."

"What are my parameters?"

"Try to stay on the right side of the law, but if you can't…" I shrugged. "Just bring me results."

Draven nodded and got to his feet. "I'll be in touch."

I escorted him back to the lobby, then returned to my office. After dropping a text to Cole to thank him for the introduction, I decided to use the time to catch up on some emails. If I went home now, so soon, Christa might think it was odd that I'd traveled into the office for a ten-minute meeting. Despite agreeing to be completely honest, I didn't want her to know I'd found a private investigator just yet. If Draven discovered something of use, then I'd tell her. Until then, I didn't see the point in getting her hopes up.

Angie arrived a few minutes after Draven had left. She virtually skidded to a stop when she spotted me sitting behind my desk.

"Mr. Somers. I didn't expect you in today."

I pointedly stared at my Rolex then turned my attention to Angie and quirked an eyebrow.

She blinked and stuttered, "Sorry I'm running late. I got stuck in traffic."

"Well, now that you are here, grab me a coffee and a bagel, please. I haven't had time for breakfast."

She nodded. "Yes, sir."

She closed the door after her with a quiet click. I could imagine her flipping the bird on the other side. If she thought my being with Christa would make me any less of a bastard in the office, I'd just firmly put her back in her place. Business and pleasure were two very different things in my book, and I intended to keep them mutually exclusive. The ability to compartmentalize my home and business life worked in my favor. Showing too much of a human side to my employees would be the start of a slippery slope. I was the boss, and it didn't do any harm to remind others of that fact from time to time.

Angie dropped off my breakfast without saying a word. I ignored her displeasure and started going through my emails. Despite checking them every day Christa and I had been away, there were a significant number that required my attention. Angie had marked them in order of importance, which made my job a little easier.

My phone pinged with a text, and when I glanced at the screen, my pulse sped up. *Christa.* I smiled.

My smile didn't remain in place for long as I read her text.

Fuck. Atwood had made his move. I messaged Paul to bring the car around the front and strode across my office. I yanked the door open. Angie's head snapped up.

"See you Monday," I said and, without further explanation, or waiting for Angie to reply, I got into the elevator and jabbed a finger at the button to take me to the lobby.

Paul was standing by the back door of the car. The second he saw me, he opened it.

"Home, please. And make it fast."

Twenty minutes later, I marched through the foyer of my penthouse. "Christa," I called out.

I found her sitting in the living room, a wad of papers on the table in front of her. Max was on the rug, playing with his toys, so entranced he didn't even notice I'd arrived home.

Christa lifted her chin, and her bottom lip trembled. "At least I'm not waiting anymore. The waiting was the worst."

I sat beside her and drew her into my arms. She felt so tiny, so frail, and yet I knew beneath her exterior was a will of iron. We sat in silence for a few moments, and I stroked her back soothingly. There were no tears, just a quiet resolve. She humbled me.

"Can I read them?" I asked.

She nodded, leaned forward to pick up the papers, then passed them to me. I scanned them, noting the date. Ten days until the first hearing. A little over a week before I came face to face with that bastard. I *must* ensure I kept my temper on a tight leash. If I showed anything other than an icy calm, it would be used against Christa, and I couldn't have that. A top lawyer like Francesca might be able to explain away one violent outburst, but showing any kind of anger in front of the judge would only play into Atwood's hands. I wouldn't make it that easy.

"I'll call Francesca," I said, sounding a lot calmer than I felt. "We'll go to see her later today."

"No," Christa said, clutching at my arm. "I don't want to leave Max."

At hearing his name, Max looked up. He grinned as he spotted me, and held out his arms. "Dada."

I swung him in the air, making him giggle, then popped him in front of his toys once more and ruffled his hair.

"Okay. I'll call and tell her to come by here instead." Considering the size of the retainer the woman was on, she could damn well make a house call.

Needing a moment alone to pull myself together, I went to my study. I rested my knuckles on the edge of my desk and stared at the gray clouds rolling in off the Hudson. Flames rose from my stomach, burning my throat. I breathed deeply, struggling to keep my anger in check. Every time I thought about what Atwood intended to do—using Max to further his own ends, with the sole intention of hurting Christa—my insides twisted with rage.

It took several minutes before I'd collected myself enough to make the call. Francesca's PA informed me she was just finishing up with a client. Agreeing to wait, I paced around my study, the terrible piped hold music grating on my nerves. There should be a way for the customer to silence the damn thing.

Five minutes later, Francesca came on the line. "Dayton. I didn't expect to hear from you so soon."

"He's filed a motion," I said. "Christa was served an hour ago."

A slight pause, then, "Okay. Quicker than I expected, but that's fine. Can you scan the papers and email them over to me?"

"Yes. I'll do it now." I fed the papers into the scanner and pressed the button. "I need you to come by my penthouse today."

She cleared her throat. "I don't usually see clients outside of the office. Is there any particular reason you can't come here?"

I clenched my jaw, irritated she'd even questioned my reasoning. "As a matter of fact, there is. Sorry if it inconveniences you," I said, sarcasm prevalent in my tone. "But considering the size of your hourly rate, not to mention the enormous retainer, I'll expect you at my home this evening."

There was an audible hitch of breath down the phone followed by the sound of a mouse clicking. "Hold on. Let me check my calendar." The line fell silent and then, "Shall we say five-thirty to six?"

"Perfect. We'll see you later."

—

Francesca arrived a few minutes before six. Christa finished up feeding Max while I fixed us all a drink. After he'd eaten, she settled him on the couch next to us. I gave him my iPad to play with, and in seconds he was chattering away to himself and giggling at a cartoon. He wouldn't be able to follow our conversation, but I still preferred his focus to be elsewhere.

"I've reviewed the papers," Francesca said. "They're as I would expect in a case like this. No court would grant anyone immediate custody, especially when the petitioner hasn't been part of the child's life up to this point. There will always be a period of visitation first, and then he'll have to come back to court at a later date when his formal custody petition will be heard." She patted Christa's knee. "So, no worrying that he'll just be able to take Max and that'll be it. There's a long road ahead, and during that time, Max will continue to live right here, where he belongs."

Christa nibbled on her thumbnail. "I don't want him to have any access at all. I can't bear the thought of Max even spending one minute alone with that man."

"He won't be alone, at least not at first. We'll request a court appointed chaperone. I'd be very surprised if the judge doesn't concur, especially given that Max and Mr. Atwood are strangers. At the end of the day, the courts are concerned with Max's welfare above all else, and whatever decisions they make will be with his best interests at heart."

"How can any contact with that man be good for my son?" Christa said through gritted teeth. "He's an animal."

I squeezed Christa's fingers while Francesca gave a sympathetic head tilt. "Not in the eyes of the law. I'm sorry, Christa, but the court will only deal in facts, and the fact is that Mr. Atwood has been completely exonerated of any wrong doing toward you. Like I explained when we met earlier in the week, we won't even be able to use that to bolster our case." She leaned forward, her forearms resting on her knees. "The best-case scenario we can hope for is that we drag this out long enough for him to lose interest, or something is unearthed that shines a different light on the proceedings. If he pushes ahead, I'm afraid the courts are liable to give him some form of custody, although exactly what that will entail depends on the judge we get."

Christa turned to me, horror etched into her face. "Oh God," she muttered, her skin turning ashen.

I slipped my arm around her shoulders and set my attention on Francesca. "Just so I'm clear, you're saying that whatever we do, Atwood is likely to be granted at least shared custody of Max."

Francesca nodded. "Unless you can prove that Max might come to some kind of harm under his care, I'm afraid that's exactly what we're looking at."

"You didn't say this on Monday." Christa's voice had increased in volume, her panic evident. "You said it would be okay."

Francesca shook her head. "No, Christa. I said that until he filed a motion, there wasn't anything to be done. I'm sorry if you feel that I've not been completely honest with you." She met my gaze. "I'll see if I can exert some influence to make sure we are allocated a judge who will be sympathetic to our point of view."

"You can do that?" I asked.

"I can try." She got to her feet, her eyes on Christa. "This is going to get very tough, Christa, and the worst thing you can do is become too emotional in court, especially if Mr. Atwood remains calm. The last thing you want to do is to appear to be a hysterical mother when the father comes across as serene and mild mannered. If you're willing, I'd like one of my senior associates to coach you before we appear in front of the judge."

Little did Francesca know that it wasn't Christa she needed to worry about—it was me. Anger swirled in my gut as I realized that whatever we did, we were fucked. My only hope was that Draven would find something in Atwood's background that proved violence toward women or kids. If he came back with anything less, or some sort of non-violent shit, like fraud, that bastard would gain permanent access to Max—and it'd break Christa.

"I'll do whatever I need to," Christa said, her voice eerily quiet.

"Good. I'll be in touch." Francesca picked up her purse and slipped it over her arm. "I'll see myself out."

She crossed the room then disappeared through the door into the foyer of my penthouse.

Christa sat there, numbly staring into space. I sensed her retreating, disconnecting from me, or the situation, or both. My terror at losing her grew as fast as a highly contagious disease spreading through my body. I clasped her hand in a desperate attempt to remind her I was there. Her fingers were cold beneath my own, and an icy chill raced through my veins.

"I'm going to bathe Max and then put him to bed," she said, tugging her hand from mine. She picked him up and settled him on her hip.

"Christa?"

Her gaze cut to mine, fear and worry swirling in the depths of her mocha irises. "What?"

"We're not losing Max. No matter what I have to do to ensure it."

She didn't reply. I watched as she left the room, an ever-so-slight stoop to her posture that hadn't been there until Francesca had shared the terrible truth of what we were facing.

I would not allow this to destroy her, or us. I didn't care what I had to do to guarantee we emerged victorious. As my thoughts turned to Atwood, I made a vow.

I'd avenge Christa—or die trying.

6

CHRISTA

A SLIVER of light finally bled through the drapes, signaling the pending dawn. Another day... another horror, no doubt. Francesca's blunt appraisal of my situation had kept me awake the entire night, my mind spinning with all manner of terrible outcomes. When Dayton had finally come to bed around one this morning, I'd pretended to be asleep. I despised that I'd done that, and I had a horrible feeling he knew I'd been faking it. The thing was, I hadn't been able to face the ensuing conversation about my insomnia. I'd worried him more than enough already.

I kept waiting for him to tell me this was all too much trouble and that he wanted out. I might have reacted hastily when Sutton had told me he intended to use Dayton's violence against Arek to support his petition. My initial reaction had been to end things between us, but that was the last thing I wanted. A knee-jerk reaction, one I'd quickly discarded. I couldn't face this alone. I needed Dayton by my side, especially when I had to face Sutton in court in nine days' time.

He deserved so much more, though. He'd been nothing but supportive, spending his hard-earned money on fancy lawyers to fix an issue that, in reality, had nothing to do with him, and for what? To end up with his good name dragged through the mud—because there wasn't a single doubt in my mind that Sutton would try to do exactly that—in order to save me. To save Max.

I hated the guilt swirling in my abdomen, but I had little choice. I needed Dayton, both financially and emotionally.

I rolled onto my side and slipped my hands beneath my head, watching him sleep. His long eyelashes graced his cheeks, his face serene in rest, the deep frown lines so visible during the daytime smoothed out.

My fingers itched to touch him, to seize the peace of mind that came from sex. When Dayton was inside me, the voices in my head quieted, and I could pretend, for an all-too-brief passage of time that everything was normal, that I wasn't about to face having to hand over my son to an evil psychopath.

I grazed my fingertips over his chest, touching the light dusting of soft hair. His breathing remained deep and slow. I snuggled into his side and pressed an open-mouthed kiss to his neck. He murmured but didn't wake. I raised myself on my elbow and traced the outline of his lips with the tip of my tongue. This time a humming noise rumbled through his chest. Sensing he was waking up, I kissed him properly, covering his body with mine. His cock grew hard, and I gently rocked my hips and rubbed my clit against him. The humming sound morphed into a full-on growl.

"Good morning," I whispered.

He held my hair away from my face. "It is now," he said, his voice raw and husky. "God, you're beautiful."

"I want you," I said, dipping down to kiss his cheek, his neck, his chest.

He groaned and tilted his pelvis, rubbing my sensitive nub. "Angel, you've got me. Whatever you need."

"I need to not think, just for a little bit."

His gaze searched mine, and I knew, without having to say another word, that he understood. It was one of the things I loved about him. We communicated verbally, physically, emotionally, psychologically. He *knew* me. I could barely believe that ten months ago, I didn't even know Dayton Somers existed, yet now, I couldn't imagine living without him for even one day.

He gripped the hem of my nightgown and lifted it over my head. His eyes grazed over me, and his hands skimmed my waist, setting my nerve endings on fire. He sat up until we were nose to nose, and his lips closed over mine, searching, exploring, taking what he needed, but giving me what I desired in return. His tongue tangled with mine, moving with deliberate strokes, sending me hurtling into ecstatic bliss.

I slipped my hand into the gap in the front of his boxers. His cock felt so hard in my hands, hot, heavy, throbbing. I brushed my thumb over the tip where pre-cum had gathered. His erection jerked in approval.

I broke off our kiss and sucked my thumb into my mouth, tasting the salty essence of him. I curved my hands around the back of his neck and threaded my fingers through his hair. "I don't want to wait."

"Then don't wait," he murmured, his eyes on mine, drawing me in.

I reached between us once more and, lifting my hips, I gripped his girth and guided him inside me. We groaned simultaneously as I slid down his entire length. I began a slow rotation of my hips, Dayton holding me with a firm grip, controlling the speed. He grew larger and harder as I rode him, our sweaty bodies writhing together, our breathing synchronized.

He shifted, increasing the pressure and angle on my clit. *Oh God.* I was so damned close. I grabbed hold of his shoulders, partly to steady myself and partly because it helped me to grind in exactly the right way. I clenched, chasing that swell that started deep within my abdomen and slowly grew upward and outward until my fingertips and toes tingled and a warm rush tore through my body.

"Look at me, Christa," Dayton commanded, his instruction impossible to ignore even though every instinct screamed at me to let my head fall back, to allow my eyes to roll inside their sockets, to focus all my attention on the peak of my climax. He cupped my face, forcing me to obey. Our gazes collided. And then I knew why he'd given such an order—because the love and adoration in his expression caused an explosion within me, the likes of which wrung me out, ravaged me, tied me to him forever. There could never be another. He'd ruined me for any other man. I was his, and he was mine.

His entire body tensed, and a strangled groan sounded low in his throat. "God, Christa." His mouth collided with mine, and his cock jerked within me, filling me up. His hands fell to my waist, and he gripped me, almost painfully. He tore his mouth away and touched our foreheads together as his climax abated, all the while muttering how much he loved me, how he couldn't live without me, how I was his everything.

I wrapped my arms around him and tucked my head into his neck as we waited for our breathing to slow and our heartbeats to return to normal. Slicked in sweat, I lifted off him and flopped onto the mattress. His hand sought mine, and he threaded our fingers together.

"I'm sorry I woke you."

He turned his head. "Angel, wake me like that every morning, and I'll be a very happy man indeed."

I chuckled. Nestling into his side, I closed my eyes. Maybe now I'd be able to fall asleep. Within a couple of minutes, Dayton's breathing changed, and his arm loosened around me. I shifted onto my back, but my hopes of rest were short-lived. Thoughts crowded my mind, and images flashed behind my closed lids of Sutton taking Max and never bringing him back. Or not looking after him properly. He wouldn't know that Max liked to snuggle while he drank his morning milk, or that he found it difficult to sleep unless his favorite bear was right beside him. Or how much he adored peanut butter and would barter for a thicker spreading on his toast. Tears pricked behind my eyes. I let them fall. Holding them back would only ensure a sore throat and a banging headache.

How had it come to this? The man who'd arranged for me to be beaten to within an inch of my life, all in an effort to force a miscarriage of a baby he didn't want. And yet now, he'd come for my precious boy with the sole intention of hurting me for having the audacity to give birth to him. My brain couldn't make sense of it. The idea of Sutton spending one second with Max created an ache in my heart which tore me apart. And yet, according to Francesca, I couldn't do a thing about it. I would have to stand by and let the person I loved more than anything in the whole world be taken from me by a man who didn't care, who only wanted to use him to further his own agenda.

Flinging back the covers, I climbed out of bed and padded across our vast bedroom. I slipped into the bathroom, silently closing the door. I switched on the light and stared at myself in the mirror. Dark smudges gave my eyes a bruised and tired look, and there was no sparkle, no light, only a dullness that spoke of the inner turmoil Sutton had created within me. I *hated* that man, with every fiber of my being. I never thought I'd be capable of such toxic thoughts and feelings. Not for the first time, regret rushed through me. I wish I'd never shown Rochelle compassion that first day when she'd been crying on the street corner because her boyfriend had dumped her. If I'd walked on by, I never would have met Sutton Atwood.

But then that also meant I wouldn't have Max, and he was the only good thing to come out of this heinous situation. Well, him and meeting Dayton, of course. But Max was my one triumph, my proudest achievement. The dichotomy of hating the very man who created the one being I loved above all else completely messed with my head.

I brushed my teeth and refreshed my face with a splash of

cold water. Feeling marginally more awake, I crept out of the bedroom. After checking on Max, I wandered into the living area. Dawn had well and truly broken, and an orange glow lightened the sky. I made a cup of coffee and took it out onto the balcony. Cars were already filling up the streets many floors below, but from up here, I couldn't hear a thing. I breathed in the peace and quiet and watched the sun rise. How could such ugliness exist in a world that was so beautiful?

I walked back inside and rinsed out my cup, leaving it to drain on the countertop. My phone rang, and I frowned. I swiftly picked it up before it woke Max or Dayton. I didn't recognize the number. It was probably one of those cold callers trying to sell me something I didn't need.

"Hello," I said, my tone reinforcing my annoyance at the early interruption.

"Hey, baby. You got the court papers then?"

My blood ran cold. I reached out to grab something, anything, to help steady me, my fingers only clutching at thin air. I managed to make it over to the couch and let my legs fall out from beneath me.

"What do you want, Sutton?" I said, furious at the slight tremor to my tone. I should have expected him to call. Of course he'd want to taunt me, to feed off my terror at the prospect of losing Max. It was how he got his pleasure—causing pain to others, especially me. He'd used a different number from when he'd called last week, again, a move I should have anticipated. He would want to catch me off guard, and if I could see it was him calling, then I'd have a chance to prepare myself. That would give me control over the situation, and Sutton would hate that. But I also knew that not answering wouldn't do me any good either. That would simply make him angrier.

"Can't I call to see how you are? I've missed you, baby."

"Fuck you, Sutton."

"Hey!" he barked. "Watch your fucking language. Remember who you're talking to."

My instincts were screaming for me to hang up, but I didn't dare. An action such as that could send him into a vicious rage, and he'd find a way to take that fury out on me. I needed to remain calm but aloof. Try not to let him see how much his actions were tearing me apart. I must remember what Francesca said. If Sutton gave an Oscar-winning performance in front of the judge, and I came across as unbalanced, Max would be the one to suffer.

"It's early. What do you want?" My voice sounded weary, even to my own ears.

"Beautiful day in New York, isn't it? I mean, wow, what a sunrise."

I froze. *He's here!* On instinct, I slowly twisted my head, peeking over my shoulder, as if I expected him to be standing right behind me.

"I didn't think I'd like it out east, but you know, I kinda do. I'm going to need a base out here, especially as my lawyer thinks it's a slam-dunk that I'll get immediate visitation rights to Max, and eventually, at the very least, joint custody is a given."

Bile rose from my stomach. I swallowed it back down, wincing at the vile taste. *Don't be sick. Hold it together. Stay calm.*

"I spoke to a realtor yesterday. There's a three-bedroom place for sale in your building. It's far from my usual standard, but it will suit my immediate needs. I'd have preferred the penthouse, but apparently it's taken." He barked out a cruel laugh. "Hi, neighbor."

The room started to spin. I jammed a fist into my mouth to stifle a scream. Sweat beaded on my forehead, and my entire body broke out in pins and needles as adrenaline filled my blood. I was trapped in a never-ending hell, forced to live eternally in the shadow of Sutton's evilness. I'd never be free, never feel safe. There was no way out of this horror except to kill myself, and I'd never do that to Max or to Dayton.

My phone fell from my grasp, clattering against the hardwood floor. The screen cracked, and the connection broke. Paralyzed, I stared into nothingness. Not only was Sutton going to take my son, but he was going to pervade every inch of my life until he sent me spiraling into madness. That had to be his ultimate aim, to have me taken away in a straightjacket and locked in a padded cell. Even then, he'd probably still find ways to torture me.

I lost track of time, but when Max's cries reached me, I struggled to my feet and plodded to his room. His sweet face greeted me, tears turning to smiles as he saw I'd come for him. My heart ached. There had to be a way out of this mess. The answer, though, eluded me.

I lifted him out of his crib and settled him on my hip. I fetched him some warm milk and flicked on the TV. He snuggled into my side, his attention stolen by the colorful cartoons. I pressed my lips to the top of his head, breathing in his smell, locking away the memories for the day when he wouldn't be by my side.

"There's my two favorite people."

I raised my head to find Dayton at the entrance to the living room, making his way over to us. I'd been so lost in my own thoughts, I hadn't heard him get up. Max wriggled off my lap and ran into Dayton's outstretched arms. He swung Max in the air then covered his face in kisses.

"Morning, little man. You hungry?"

"Yep."

"Then let's get you fed."

His eyes cut to mine. I smiled but from the way Dayton's brow furrowed, it hadn't reached my eyes. I shook my head in silent communication. He nodded in understanding.

Dayton made pancakes, eggs, and bacon—Mrs. Connor, his

housekeeper, only worked part-time—and I joined him and Max at the table to eat. Despite my best efforts, my throat had closed up, and after forcing down a couple of mouthfuls, I dropped my fork and pushed my plate away. Dayton's worried expression tore at my heart. He'd be just as hurt by the ease with which Sutton could get to me.

Dayton cleared away the breakfast things while I sat Max in front of the TV. I cocked my head at Dayton. He followed me onto the balcony, frowning.

"Sutton called me this morning."

Fury swept across his face, his ice-blue eyes darkening in anger. "He fucking what?" he said between clenched teeth, a nerve ticking in his cheek.

"He's buying an apartment in this building."

Dayton's eyes widened. "No he fucking isn't," he shouted, loud enough that Max twisted his head. He soon turned back to the TV, thankfully.

"Keep your voice down," I hissed.

"I will *not* allow that bastard to live in this building. Not happening, Christa. The thought of you bumping into him every time you come home…" He shuddered. "I'll buy the damned building before I'll let that happen."

"Dayton, don't be ridiculous. You can't buy the building. It'd cost a fortune."

His face changed. Instead of my boyfriend, the man I loved standing in front of me, I was hit with Dayton Somers, CEO, fearsome businessman, the guy who always got what he wanted. The Dayton Somers who'd sent fear rushing through me the first day I'd met him, urging me to run. Fortunately, he'd allowed me to see the man behind the public face, but dear God, when he donned that persona, he was formidable.

"Watch me."

7

DAYTON

"LION!" Max bounced on top of my shoulders when he spotted the magnificent animal prowling around its enclosure. The female of the species was lounging against a fence, enjoying the sunshine, a couple of cubs playing nearby. "Closer."

I stole a glance at Christa. She was putting on one hell of a show for Max, excitedly chattering as we walked around the zoo, but I knew her mind was elsewhere. Hardly surprising given Atwood's unsolicited call that morning. I wanted to kill the man with my bare hands for the pain and suffering he gleefully inflicted on Christa. I might not be able to do that, but I could stop the fucker from buying a home in our building.

Before we'd set off for the zoo, I'd called the head of the condominium association for my building, a man I knew well and had had several business dealings with over the years. After I updated him on the reason for my call, he not only passed on the contact details of the seller, but also promised that if any other apartments came up for sale, he'd let me know. That way, I could snap up the apartment immediately. Properties in my particular building rarely came onto the market, but at least this way, I'd be able to put a stop to any future attempts.

My second call was to the current owner of the apartment that Atwood thought he was buying. We agreed on a price—an inflated price. I'd been fleeced. The owner knew it, and I knew it, but it didn't matter. If it had been a business deal, I'd have nailed the guy to the wall by his balls, but this was personal.

Atwood only had one reason for trying to buy an apartment where we lived, and that was to heap more misery upon Christa.

Bad luck, asshole. You failed.

If only the custody battle over Max could be solved so easily. That, I feared, was going to get a lot worse before it got any better, and the eventual outcome was outside my sphere of influence. I *hated* not being in control. It reminded me of being forced to leave Nina behind when I was sixteen, and the feelings of hopelessness that I'd had to find a way to deal with. I despised anything that reminded me of that time.

"Shall we get some lunch," I suggested when Max's excited chattering faded, his energy expended—for the time being at least. It wouldn't be long until he was bouncing around again.

"Do you mind if we go home?" Christa asked.

I draped an arm around her shoulder and kissed her hair. "Whatever you want, angel. It's exhausting, pretending, isn't it?"

She met my concerned gaze, then rested her head against me. "I love you. Don't ever leave me, please."

I chuckled. "You won't get rid of me that easily."

"Thank goodness for that."

It took us an hour to get home, by which time Max was over-hungry and showed his displeasure by wailing at the top of his lungs as we crawled the last two miles. The old me, pre-Christa, would have been irritated, but now, my only concern was to make him feel comfortable again. How I'd changed, and for the better.

We got him fed and settled, then grabbed a bite to eat ourselves. Thankfully, Christa ate her entire sandwich. I'd expected a battle. Every time her stress levels increased, Christa lost her appetite, and the last few weeks had definitely taken their toll.

Her phone rang, and I watched the blood drain from her face.

"Is it him?"

"I don't know. It's not the same number as this morning."

"Give it to me," I commanded.

She didn't hesitate, pushing the phone across the kitchen table. I tapped the cracked screen to answer.

"Somers," I barked down the line.

"Hello, sir. I'm calling to see if you would be interested in our new travel booking service. I—"

I hung up. "Cold caller." When she sagged with relief, I took her hands in mine. "I think we should change your number. We need to get you a new cell anyway, so we could do that at the same time."

She shook her head. "It wouldn't work. He'd find out the new one in no time. Besides," she said, shrugging, "if he can't get hold of me, it'll only make him worse, more hurtful, angrier." My face must have shown I disagreed, because Christa continued. "Trust me on this. I know Sutton. If I make myself inaccessible, it'll only fuel his rage, not to mention the courts will probably expect him to be able to contact me, especially if he gets some form of visitation."

I didn't like it, but I had to succumb to her superior knowledge when it came to that fucker. And she was right about the court.

"True," I said grudgingly. "But let's continue to reassess."

My phone rang. Draven. I snatched it up.

"Sorry, angel, I need to take this." I strode out of the living room. Luckily, Christa didn't find my behavior strange as I often took business calls in my study.

"Any news?" I asked the second I closed the door behind me.

"I arrived in Seattle this morning, and I've started to make a few inquiries but nothing to report so far."

I expelled an irritated breath. "Results, Draven. That's what I need. Fast results."

"It's early days, man," Draven replied. I had the distinct impression he dealt with demanding people like me on a regular basis, if his patient response was anything to go by. "You gotta understand that this could take a while, and that's if there's any shit to dig out."

I breathed noisily through my nose. "Trust me, it's there, and I'm relying on you to find it." I knew I was being unreasonable. I'd only hired the guy yesterday morning, but that wouldn't stop me from pushing him hard. If I remained constantly on his back, he'd work harder. Fact.

"I feel you. I'll check in again tomorrow."

———

The morning of the initial hearing finally arrived. As each day had passed, Christa had withdrawn farther into her shell. She still turned up to work and, according to my sources, continued to perform to the highest levels, her coworkers completely unaware of the turmoil in her private life. But the light-hearted, teasing, fun-loving girl I loved morphed into an introspective shadow of her former self. She didn't need to voice her concerns about coming face to face with Atwood. The last time she'd set eyes on him had been at his sentencing hearing ten months earlier, and she'd rightfully assumed that would be the last time she'd ever have to see him. Unfortunately, a few greased palms had set a monster free, and Christa was the one to suffer.

Apart from finding a couple of exes who hadn't exactly spoken highly of Atwood, and a few dodgy dealings, Draven hadn't come up with anything I could use to help fight our corner. The lack of progress was driving me crazy. There *had* to be something dark hidden in his past. Something I could use to blackmail the bastard into backing the fuck off. But he was either extraordinarily adept at covering his own tracks, or there wasn't any dirt to find. I didn't believe either scenario.

Our babysitter, Mrs. Flannigan—who'd turned into something of a godsend and was someone I'd been seriously thinking about putting on the payroll—arrived to take care of Max. Christa took some persuading to leave him, while a bemused Max couldn't understand why his mother kept coming back for another kiss and a hug. The more I watched her inner turmoil play out, the more my anger grew. I felt like a rabid dog had chewed on my insides, such was the constant fire burning in my abdomen.

Paul stopped the car outside the family court building. I spotted Francesca waiting outside. When I turned to Christa, I found her pale and slightly clammy, and she was repeatedly gnawing on her bottom lip and twisting the strap on her purse.

"It's going to be okay, angel," I said, tucking a lock of hair behind her ear.

She raised her eyes to mine. "I don't think anything will ever be okay again after today."

My heart squeezed painfully. There was nothing I could say that would comfort her or make this horror disappear. All I could do was be there and try to deflect the bullets as they were fired.

"I'm here," I said, taking her hand. "Lean on me."

We stepped onto the sidewalk. Francesca spotted us and came over.

"All set?" she asked.

Christa gave Francesca a tired smile. "We're pretty tense as it is. I'm sure you can understand."

Francesca nodded. "I do." She patted Christa's shoulder. "Okay, let's do this."

She spun on her heel and walked inside. We followed her into the courthouse. She'd already briefed us on what would happen today, and Christa had spent an hour or so with one of Francesca's team members preparing her for what was to come.

Francesca didn't expect it to be a long hearing. Both sides had already submitted their papers. Atwood's petition claimed access to Max and, as expected, he'd cited my violent altercation with Kawalski as a reason why a more permanent arrangement should be considered at the earliest convenience. We'd obviously issued a firm rebuttal, to both the visitation and the permanent residence application. Francesca had told us to prepare for the judge granting Atwood immediate access. Walking inside the courthouse, it felt like a pointless exercise in futility.

The inside of the building smelled of despair, of angst, of anger and frustration. I gripped Christa's hand tighter, the sound of her heels echoing in the wide, high-ceilinged hallway. We turned a corner, and Christa pulled up fast. I followed her gaze. Atwood was lounging against a wall, his feet casually crossed at the ankles, tapping on his phone. Beside him was a woman, definitely family if the resemblance was anything to go by, and another guy, likely his lawyer.

"Easy, angel." I steered Christa to a seat as far away from Atwood as we could get. "Shouldn't they be waiting somewhere else?" I hissed at Francesca.

She gave me an apologetic shrug and a half-grimace. Atwood raised his chin, his eyes on Christa, and he smiled. The bastard actually smiled. I clenched my hand into a fist, the one that wasn't holding Christa's, desperately trying to offer her some comfort. What I wouldn't give to go over there and wipe that smile off his goddamn face.

His companion flashed a look of pure hatred in Christa's direction. Atwood, by comparison, kept his face arranged in a genial expression as he pushed off the wall and walked toward us. Christa sucked in a breath, and her entire body stiffened.

"Dayton," she whispered, her voice trembling.

She didn't need to say anything else. I got to my feet, standing in front of Christa, and held up my hand. "Not another step."

Atwood's forehead wrinkled in an attempt at conveying confusion. "I only want to say hello to the mother of my child."

I clenched my jaw, a hundred curse words swimming around my head. My absolute helplessness to protect her was *killing* me. "She doesn't want to talk to you," I said icily. "Now fuck off."

Francesca stood and put a hand on my arm in warning. "Mr. Atwood, I suggest you take a seat at the far end of the waiting area. This is a difficult time for all of us."

Atwood shrugged, his smirk still firmly in place, but behind his eyes, the malevolence briefly rose to the surface. I'd known this guy had evil stamped all the way through to his rotten core, but knowing and seeing were two completely different things. I straightened my posture, rising to my full height, and fixed my gaze on him, my message clear. *You don't fucking scare me.*

He strolled back to his side of the waiting room where his lawyer spoke to him in rapid, low tones, probably telling him to stay away. Atwood appeared bored, staring into the distance, barely listening.

I sat beside Christa and twisted my body so that Atwood, and the woman whose hateful stare burned into the back of my head, wouldn't be able to see her. "It's okay, angel. Breathe. This will soon be over."

"And then I'll have to hand Max over to him, won't I?" she said, the pain in her voice tugging at my heartstrings.

I wouldn't disrespect her by disagreeing, because we both knew we'd lose this first round. We just had to get it over with and then work on our strategy for preventing more permanent access. Draven mightn't have found jack shit, but I remained stoic in my belief the dirt was there, and if we remained tenacious and focused, we'd find it.

The door to the courtroom opened, and we were invited inside by the official. Christa clung to my hand, but she kept her posture erect, her eyes facing forward. She took a seat beside Francesca. I sat on the bench directly behind their table.

Suppressing the urge to send a vengeful glare in Atwood's direction, I formed my face into a bland expression, one that I'd used in the boardroom and during business negotiations on several very successful occasions. No one looking at me would guess at the vortex of emotions swirling in my gut.

The whole procedure was over in less than ten minutes. As expected, Atwood received visitation rights, although I took it as a minor victory that he only got one two-hour visit with Max per week for the next two weeks, the first one of which would be tomorrow, after which the judge wanted us back in court to reassess. Francesca successfully argued for a court-appointed chaperone to accompany Max, and the slight bend to Christa's spine at that news told of her relief that Atwood wouldn't be left alone with her son.

The second the judge left the courtroom. I jumped from my seat and grabbed Christa's hand. I hustled her to the exit, but halfway down the hallway, Atwood caught up to us. He must have run on ahead because he was alone.

"Round one to me," he said, sneering.

Christa trembled in my arms, but my chest swelled with pride when she fixed her attention on me and said, "Shall we go home," as though Atwood hadn't even spoken.

I smiled down at her and tucked her closer into my side. "Whatever my angel wants."

We'd almost reached the exit when Atwood called out, "See you soon, Sienna, especially when I'm living two floors down."

A grin inched across my face. The current owner mustn't have broken the news yet. It would be such a shame not to take this opportunity to inform him of the change in circumstance. I turned around, very deliberately, and locked gazes with him. "Firstly, her name is Christa, except *you* can call her Ms. Adams. And secondly, I think you'll find that apartment is no longer for sale."

A frown drew his brows low, giving him a sullen, almost

childlike appearance. "What the fuck are you talking about, Somers?"

My lips curled into a smug smile. "A better offer came along."

"Dayton," Francesca said in a warning tone.

I ignored her. By now, both Atwood's lawyer and his female companion, who Christa had whispered to me earlier on was his sister, had caught up with him. Excellent. They might as well all hear this.

"I'll use lots of small words to make this easy for you to understand. If you struggle, I'm sure your lawyer can translate. I'm the new owner of that apartment, and every other apartment in that building that might come up for sale in the future." I took a couple of steps in his direction until we were toe to toe. I glared down at him. This bastard wasn't the only one who could instill fear in people, except I chose to fight my battles in the boardroom rather than beat defenseless, pregnant women half to death. I internally high-fived myself when Atwood stepped back. I lowered my voice. "Round fucking two to me, asshole."

I spun on my heel, took hold of Christa's hand, and swept her outside.

8

CHRISTA

DAYTON SLIPPED his arms around my waist and rested his chin on my shoulder. I leaned into his comforting embrace and tried to absorb his strength into my body. Today was undoubtedly going to be one of the toughest days of my life. I felt so powerless, caught up in a system that professed to only want the best for Max, and yet would happily send him off into the arms of a psychopath. How I'd kept it together yesterday, I'd never know. I smiled, though, every time I thought back to when Dayton had told Sutton he wouldn't be living in our building. I didn't want to think about how much it had cost Dayton to win that victory for me, but he insisted buying Manhattan real estate was a good investment. Not for the first time, I wondered what I would have done, how I'd have fought Sutton if not for Dayton's enormous wealth.

"How are you holding up? Get much sleep?"

I shook my head. "Not a wink."

"Me either." He kissed the top of my head. "Max not awake yet?"

I shook my head. "I'll wake him in a little while." I turned in his arms and clutched his biceps. "Thank you. For yesterday. For everything."

He bent his head and brushed his lips over mine. "I wish I had the power to stop this from happening. I hate that you're having to go through this."

His face twisted, and I knew he was in as much pain as me. In a strange way, I took comfort in that. He understood, which meant I didn't have to pretend this wasn't tearing me apart inside, that handing Max over in a couple of hours wouldn't break me in a way I feared I'd never be able to fix.

"There is something you can do."

"Name it, angel."

"Hold me."

His eyes softened, and his hand came around the back of my head. He nestled me against his chest, and we stood there in silence while the sun rose above the high-rise buildings and New York came to life far below us.

By the time I got Max up, dressed, and fed, I was operating on autopilot. If I allowed myself to think about the reality of handing Max over, I would probably pack a bag and run as far away as I could with my son. But that wouldn't achieve anything. I had to face this, to fight it, to trust that Dayton and Francesca would do everything in their power to minimize the damage Sutton inflicted. I could only hope that Max and I came out the other side relatively unscathed. I kept thinking I'd failed as a mother. I was the one person who was supposed to protect Max and yet I couldn't shield him from this. At least the chaperone would make sure he came to no harm. I didn't think for one second Sutton would hurt him physically—he wasn't stupid —but he was a master manipulator, a man who burrowed inside people's heads and made them think they were the ones at fault.

"Okay, here we go," Dayton said when he received notification that they were on their way up.

We waited in the foyer, Dayton clutching my hand as I

clung to Max who was more than bemused by our strange behavior. I'd tried to explain to him that an old friend of Mommy's was coming to take him somewhere fun for a couple of hours. Max, being the good-natured kid he was, had simply accepted it without question. On the one hand, I wanted him to scream and yell, to throw a tantrum and refuse to go, and then the chaperone would be able to report back to the court how distressed Max was, and maybe that would go in my favor. On the other hand, I didn't want Max to suffer or be scared about what was happening. His welfare and happiness were my only concerns.

My own agony would have to be put on the back burner, at least until Sutton had left with... God, I couldn't even say the words. My breathing escalated, and I broke out in a cold sweat. Why was this happening to me? I was a good person... Wasn't I? Sutton should be rotting in jail, far away from here. He should be having to barter with cigarettes and dope to avoid becoming the bitch of some tattooed giant. Hatred filled my veins. That was exactly where he should be, living every day in fear of being raped or beaten or worse. He deserved to suffer for what he'd done to me then, and what he was putting me through now.

"Christa?"

Dayton's voice came at me through a fog of cotton wool. My neck felt stiff and sore as I looked up at him. Something in my eyes must have given me away because his face crumpled.

"Oh, angel."

He kissed my temple and tenderly brushed a lock of hair off Max's forehead. The gentleness he used on me and my son almost sent me over the edge.

The elevator pinged. I held my breath as the doors smoothly opened. Sutton strode out first, the court-appointed chaperone trailing behind, a stick-thin woman in her late forties, early fifties, with wispy gray hair tied up in a loose bun. She did have a kindly face, though. I prayed that she'd be able to see through

Sutton's façade, that she wouldn't be taken in by the charm I knew he could turn on when it suited him.

I crouched to Max's level. "Max, this is the friend of Mommy's that I told you about," I said, every word cutting through me. My tongue felt too big for my mouth, and my throat was full of razorblades. "His name is Sutton, and he's going to take you out for a couple of hours. And this lady is his friend." I didn't know how else to describe her.

"Wendy," she helpfully added.

"Hey, Max," Sutton said, crouching as he held out a stuffed animal. "I brought you this."

Max's little face lit up. "Lion," he said, reaching for it. "Momma, look."

I forced my face into a smile. "He's just like the ones we saw at the zoo, huh, Max?"

"There's plenty more where that came from," Sutton said. "We're going to have a lot of fun today, Max. In fact, we're going to be seeing a lot more of each other from now on."

I could sense the tension rolling off Dayton, the heat from his anger burning like a furnace. Max shot me a puzzled look. I glared at Sutton.

Dayton took Max from me. "Come on, Max. Let's go fetch your backpack while Mommy talks to her *friend*."

"Okay, Dada."

Sutton's eyes widened. I shot him a glare that must have spoken volumes because he kept his mouth shut, very unlike him. I waited until Dayton had gone inside, and then I turned on Sutton.

"You're confusing him," I hissed. "I only told him about today, not any future visits."

"Well, you should have," Sutton said, taking a step in my direction.

I held my ground. He couldn't hurt me here, with the court official standing right beside him and Dayton a mere few seconds away. "You'd better get used to what's going on here, Sienna, because he's my son, and I have a right to see him and spend time with him, no matter what you and your *boyfriend* think. And another thing, I'd advise you to tell Max pretty damn quick that your fuck buddy is *not h*is father. If you don't, I will."

"Don't you dare!" I spat, poking my finger in his direction. "You wanted nothing to do with him, so don't you come around here pretending to play the loving father. You belong in jail, Sutton. Far, far away from me and my son."

Wendy cleared her throat. "Why don't we all calm down?"

I ignored her. "You can pretend in front of Wendy, the judge, your lawyer, but I know you. You might be giving the performance of your life pretending you give a shit about Max, but remember, I know the truth. And the truth will come out… You mark my words."

The affronted expression he sent in my direction forced a laugh from my chest, but before our argument could continue, Dayton returned with Max in tow. He was wearing his favorite Minions backpack and clutched the lion Sutton had brought.

Sutton held out his hand and smiled at Max. "Ready to go, buddy?"

Max nodded, but as he tilted his head back and his beautiful eyes settled on mine, his chin wobbled.

Putting aside all my anger, all my hate, I crouched and kissed the top of his head. "You're going to have a fantastic time with Sutton and Wendy, Max. When you get back, I want to hear all about it, okay?"

My brave boy nodded. Sutton took Max's hand and walked away with my son. I held it together until the elevator doors closed, and then I broke down. My knees buckled, and Dayton caught me. He swept me up into his arms and carried me through to the living room. I sobbed, my face buried in his neck, as he gently laid me down on the couch.

He let me cry it out, saying nothing, doing nothing other than occasionally rocking me, as if I, too, was a child. After a few minutes, I pulled myself together, blew my nose on a tissue Dayton produced from his pocket, and dried my eyes.

"I'm okay," I said, my gaze falling on his concerned face. "I just needed to get that out. But he'll be fine. Wendy is with him, and she's hardly going to let anything bad happen, is she? Besides, it's two hours. I can do two hours." I got to my feet and paced, biting the skin around my thumbnail. "Two hours will pass by like that." I clicked my fingers, then shot a look in Dayton's direction, searching for reassurance. "Won't it?"

Dayton came to stand beside me. He caressed my face, his touch so soft and tender that more tears came. "It will."

Two hours did not pass quickly. In fact, every minute might as well have been a day. I didn't know how I was going to do this all over again next week. Agony spread through my chest every single second my son was with that monster. An hour and fifty minutes after Max had left with Sutton, I decamped to the entranceway, my eyes fixed on the elevator, waiting for the comforting sound of its arrival. Dayton waited with me, his arm around my trembling shoulders.

"I love you," I said, because I didn't say it nearly enough. I wanted him to know that his quiet reassurance the last two hours hadn't gone unnoticed. "I don't know what I'd do if you weren't by my side."

He tightened his hold and kissed my hair. "You're amazing. Strong, resilient, beautiful. Max is so lucky to have you as his mom, and I thank God every day that you're in my life. It kills me that I can't fix this for you, that I can't take away your pain, but I'll always be here. Always."

Before I could tell him how every word he said gave me a little more strength, the elevator arrived. It seemed to take forever for the doors to open, but when they did, and Max was standing there next to Sutton with a big beaming smile on his face, adrenaline rushed through me, sending me lightheaded. My baby was okay.

I bent down and held out my arms. Max sprinted toward me and threw his arms around my neck, his excitement palpable. He chattered at me, telling me all about his new best friend, Sutton, and how he'd taken him to lots of places and bought him toys and candy. I met Sutton's gaze over the top of my son's head. He was staring at me, his eyes cold, dead almost, like a great white shark's. I shuddered.

"Max, why don't you go with Dayton while I talk to Sutton," I said, careful not to use the term 'Dada.' The last thing I needed was Sutton having another hissy fit.

Sutton bent down, resting on one knee, and held out his arms to Max. My heart squeezed, and not in a good way, when Max hugged him.

"See you next week, buddy, just like we talked about," Sutton said.

"Bye," Max said, happily taking Dayton's hand.

Dayton and I locked eyes. His expression said it all. He wanted to kill Sutton at least as much as I did. I waited until they'd disappeared, then I lifted my chin and glared at Wendy.

"Is he allowed to do that?" I asked. "Surely it should be up to me to talk to my son about what's happening."

"Except you haven't, have you?" Sutton said before Wendy could even open her mouth. That faux aggrieved look he'd perfected clawed at my last remaining nerve. "All I want is to see my son, Sienna. To have him know me, and to know I made him."

I clenched my fists. How I didn't punch him remained a mystery. I could see in his eyes the game he was playing, and boy had he mastered it. I should have remained aloof, but my brain was a few seconds behind my tongue.

"My name is Christa, you sorry excuse for a human being. I stopped being Sienna the day you sent that guy to my apartment. You remember, the guy you paid who almost killed me, who nearly made me miscarry. And let me be clear: you didn't make Max, Sutton. You fucked me one night—badly as I recall—and the condom broke." I poked myself in the chest. "I made him. I brought him up. I struggled to make sure he had a roof over his head and food on the table. Me! I did all those things."

"With my money, according to Rochelle," he drawled, turning his attention to Wendy. "I hope you're logging how difficult *Christa* is making this for me. I want it noted for the record that I have been completely exonerated of any wrongdoing toward her, and the only reason I haven't been a part of my son's life until now is because *she* had me arrested and I spent almost a year in jail for a crime I didn't commit."

I barked out a bitter laugh. "Oh, you're good, Sutton. Real smooth."

He was standing slightly in front of Wendy, so she missed the faint glimmer of a smile that reeked of triumph.

"I'll see you next week, *Christa*. Give Max a kiss from me."

He strolled into the elevator, Wendy in tow, his trademark swagger sending red-hot fury racing through my veins. This time, he stood slightly behind the court chaperone, and as the doors closed, he blew me a kiss.

I rammed a fist into my mouth because if I hadn't, I'd have screamed. I felt trapped, backed into a corner, forced into this terrible situation. Realization rained down on me. I'd never break free of Sutton Atwood. We were inextricably linked.

The only escape would be death.

9

DAYTON

"As you can see from the court-appointed chaperone's report, Your Honor, Max has shown no signs of distress during the last two visits. In fact, he continues to build a very positive relationship with his father. At this time, I would like to move for a more formal arrangement, including overnight visitation until such time as the court is willing to accept a petition for custody by Mr. Atwood."

"Over my fucking dead body," I muttered under my breath, glaring at the back of Atwood's head. "Or preferably yours."

Francesca glanced over her shoulder and widened her eyes. Clearly she'd heard me. I returned her reproachful stare with an unapologetic one of my own. This wasn't an unexpected outcome, but I hated it all the same. Christa remained stoic, silent, elegantly sitting with her hands in her lap accepting a horrendous fate. The thought of Max not sleeping in his own bedroom, the idea of waking the next morning and not being able to cuddle him, play with him, watch as he licked every trace of maple syrup off his fingers… It slayed me.

Judge Houghton nodded and bent his head to make a few

notes. I got the impression he wasn't unsympathetic to Christa's cause but was penned into a corner by the law of the land.

"If it helps the court, Your Honor," Atwood's pompous—if brilliant, I grudgingly admitted—lawyer continued, "I'd like to bring to your attention at this time Mr. Atwood's continued concern for his son's current living arrangements."

I snapped my head to the left. *Oh, here it comes.* Francesca held a hand behind her back, a signal for me to be quiet, to remain composed. I'd anticipated this move. In fact, I was surprised Atwood hadn't made a point of bringing it to the judge's attention earlier. It had been in the court papers, but I guessed he'd just been biding his time. Francesca was prepped with a rebuttal; I had to trust her professional acumen.

"As you are aware, and as we have already petitioned, a business associate of Mr. Atwood's was subjected to a violent and unprovoked attack by Mr. Somers, Ms. Adams' boyfriend whose home she and Max reside within. I would like the court to note that we believe this puts Max in harm's way, and as such, move for the court to instruct the immediate removal of Max from the home of Mr. Somers."

I clenched my hands into fists, and I had to clamp my jaw shut before I said something I wouldn't regret, but that would add credence to Atwood's claims. I swallowed the growing anger burning through my gut, when all I wanted to do was send the flames hurtling into Atwood's face.

Francesca got to her feet. "Your Honor, I have here a set of sworn statements from several attendees at the function where this event occurred. Each one of these statements testifies that Mr. Kawalski, the gentleman in question, called Ms. Adams a whore, as well as acting in a very threatening manner toward her. While Mr. Somers' response to such vile commentary cannot be condoned, I'm sure the court understands his reaction to protect Ms. Adams' reputation. This is especially poignant when this heinous word was, in fact, scored onto Ms. Adams' stomach during a vicious assault for which a man is currently serving a significant prison sentence and a crime for which Mr. Atwood himself was originally convicted of commissioning—"

Atwood's lawyer leaped to his feet. "Objection, Your Honor."

"Although Mr. Atwood has since been fully exonerated of any wrongdoing," Francesca added.

I suppressed a grin. Fucking amazing lawyer. I could have kissed her. Although she shouldn't have done it, once heard, never forgotten.

"Be careful, Ms. Hale," Judge Houghton warned.

"My apologies, Your Honor. I would also like to add that each of these witnesses have provided glowing character references for Mr. Somers, a man who is a well-respected member of the Manhattan business community, and who provides gainful and worthwhile employment for a significant number of American citizens. Therefore, I would put to the court that Max is exactly where he should be, with his mother and Mr. Somers, a man who has been like a father to Max for almost a year."

Oh, she's better than amazing. With considerable effort, I managed to keep a triumphant grin from inching across my face, but I wouldn't pretend it was easy. I cut my gaze to the judge.

Atwood's lawyer scrambled to his feet. "Your Hon—"

"Sit down, Mr. Brandon. I've listened to the arguments on both sides and I have sympathy for both parents. However, my primary concern, and the concern of this court, is for Max and only Max." He fixed his attention on Christa.

I held my breath.

"Ms. Adams, it's clear to me that you are a wonderful and caring mother, and as such I have no intention, at this time, of removing Max from his loving home. However," he continued as Christa's shoulders sagged in relief, "his father has the right to spend time with his son. Therefore, my decision is that Max will spend every third weekend with his father, starting this coming weekend, as well as one day per week." He looked over at Atwood. "All visitations are to take place within the state of New York. I am aware your permanent residency is in Seattle, Mr. Atwood, but I want to make it very clear that Max is not to be removed from this state without the express approval of the court. At this time, I am not inclined to approve such a petition."

"Absolutely, Your Honor," Atwood said. "I am already in the process of buying a permanent home here in New York. It's taking me a little longer than planned as my original purchase fell through." He twisted his head and met my gaze. I sneered in response, although I did have an inkling of surprise that he hadn't tried to call me out in front of the judge. Then again, he'd sound rather petulant, and I'd already prepped Francesca with my reasoning. Manhattan real estate was a good investment, right?

The judge turned his attention back to Christa. "While you are free to travel with Max within the continental US, Ms. Adams, any international trips will require similar approval from the court. Understood?"

"Yes, Your Honor," Christa said, her voice coming across strong and clear despite the blow—albeit not an unexpected one —of the weekend visits.

"Ms. Hale, please ensure the statements you referred to are filed with the court."

Francesca inclined her head. "Already submitted, Your Honor."

Judge Houghton nodded, then rose from his seat and left the courtroom. I shot around to Christa and caught her trembling hand. "Let's go, angel," I said, keen to get her away from Atwood and his vile sister who hadn't taken her eyes off Christa the whole time we'd been in court. "I'll call you," I added to Francesca.

We were halfway toward the exit when Atwood called out

Christa's name. I spun around, shielding her with my body. "You got what you wanted, now fuck off," I said.

Atwood held his hands in the air. "Whoa there, buddy. I just want to talk to Christa, for Max's sake."

I let go of Christa's hand, despite her desperately trying to hold on, and stepped right up to Atwood. I had an inch or so on him, and I used it to the greatest effect, thrusting out my chest and narrowing my eyes. Rage hissed through my body, the same anger that boiled up every time I came into contact with this worthless piece of shit. One day, I'd find a way to exact the proper revenge on him, but today was not that day.

"Firstly," I gritted out, "I am not your *buddy*. Secondly, you don't get to talk to Christa. You don't get to even breathe the same air as her. You act like you care about Max." I snorted. "You couldn't give a shit about him. But I'm warning you. If you harm a single hair on Christa's or Max's heads, I'll make you sorrier than you ever thought possible."

A malicious sneer curled Atwood's lips. "Is that a threat?" He glanced over at his lawyer. "You got that, right?"

"Dayton, come on." Christa tugged on my arm once more. "Let's go, please."

"Yeah, it's a threat." The red mist had truly descended. My vision blurred, and a roaring sound thundered through my ears. "Watch your fucking back, Atwood. I'm coming for you."

He barked a laugh. "I look forward to it, Somers. Just remember, she and I have something you don't have. A child. That connects us in a way you can't understand. You may not like it, *buddy*, but you'd better learn to live with it." He leaned around me. "We need to talk, Christa. I'll wait until your guard dog isn't around."

I made a fist, but as much as I wanted to break his face, the practical corner of my brain knew I'd be playing right into his hands. Atwood grabbed his sister by the elbow and steered her outside. She managed to send a final hateful glare at Christa who, sensibly, kept her gaze fixed to the floor. The door to the courtroom slammed shut.

"Dayton, please," Christa pleaded once they'd gone. "I just want to go home."

Francesca glowered at me. "Well done, Dayton. Next time, keep your thoughts to yourself." She swept past us and disappeared through the same door as Atwood.

I raked a hand through my hair. "Shit. Sorry, angel." I sank onto a nearby bench at the back of the courtroom. "I hate this. I hate him. I can't bear what this is doing to you. To us. I want to kill him, Christa. Every single time I see his smug face, I want to beat him into the ground until he doesn't get back up." I covered my face with my hands and rubbed hard. "I thought I hated my father, but it's nothing in comparison with the feelings I have about Atwood. I can't control them. I don't know what to do."

I met her worried gaze as she sat beside me. She linked her arm through mine and rested her head on my shoulder. "The only thing you have to do, Dayton, is be there, and you have been. You are. I've told you before, I couldn't do this without you. You're my tower of strength, my life raft on a stormy sea, my rock to cling on to. I understand the rage, the hatred, the anger, how powerless you feel, because I feel all those things, too. I don't want Sutton anywhere near Max, but it's out of my hands, and if I don't find a way to come to terms with it, to make peace with how things are until Max is old enough to make up his own mind, I'll go mad."

I kissed the top of her head. "I understand. Really, I do, and I will support your decisions, whatever they are. But I'm not you. I can't simply accept the fact that a man who brutalized you, who almost ensured that Max never existed, who made you feel fear and anguish and worry—and is still making you feel all those things—is going to be a part of our lives for the foreseeable future. I owe it to you to be completely honest and that's why I have to tell you that I'll continue searching for something that will get that man out of our lives for good. I'll never stop until he's gone."

She raised her head and met my gaze, then lifted her hand and caressed my face. "And I love you for it," she said. "Now can we please go home. I want to spend the rest of the day with Max and the night in your arms."

I covered her hand with my own and smiled. "I can't think of anything better."

10

CHRISTA

I locked my computer, picked up my purse, slotted my phone in my jacket pocket, and headed for the elevators. My heart seemed to leap into my throat and my stomach landed somewhere around my feet, making for a truck load of discomfort. I *had* to do this. I hated lying to Dayton, but it was for the best. That was why I'd told him I was meeting Joanna—the lady who ran the local parenting group—for lunch. Guilt settled heavily on my shoulders at his obvious pleasure that I was making friends, but I had no choice. If he found out I was meeting Sutton, he'd go crazy.

Sutton had texted me the night of the court hearing, reiterating his request for us to talk. Unlike the Sutton I knew—and despised—his text had sounded almost convivial. I didn't trust him for one second but figured he wouldn't leave me alone until I gave him his platform. Best to get it over with, and then the only time I'd have to see him would be when he picked up Max and dropped him off.

I'd chosen the meeting place, a busy coffee shop a few minutes' walk from my office. I slipped inside and stood in line at the counter. Sutton hadn't arrived yet, but as I was five minutes early, I wasn't surprised. At least it gave me a chance to get settled and prepare myself for having to sit across from the man who'd hurt me so badly, emotionally and physically, and still continued to heap more misery upon me. Whatever transpired, I mustn't let him rile me. I had to stay calm. If he saw an open wound, he'd poke at it. That was Sutton's way. He couldn't help himself.

I chose a seat at the back, facing the door, and waited. Right on cue, Sutton arrived. My pulse sped up, the skin at the back of my neck prickled, and sweat slicked my palms. I wiped them on my skirt. *Calm down, Christa.* He couldn't hurt me in a public place. The only thing he had in his power was to use cruel, hateful words, and I struggled to think of a single thing he could say that he hadn't said before.

His gaze fell on me, and when he spotted a single cup of coffee resting on the table, he arched an eyebrow, then stood in line. Five minutes later, he sauntered over holding a large latte and took the seat opposite. I'd purposely set my purse on the seat next to mine, sending a clear message. *Stay the hell back.*

"I guess I shouldn't have expected you to get me a drink," he said, tearing open a pack of sugar and tipping it into his coffee.

"I think you can afford your own, Sutton," I said.

He smirked as he stirred in the sugar, his attention on his cup. He set the spoon on the table then picked up his drink and raised his eyes to gaze at me over the rim. "Your guard dog not with you?"

I mashed my lips together, ignoring his dig at Dayton. If he knew who I'd intended to have lunch with, he'd have insisted on coming along which would have significantly increased the chances of an altercation.

"You asked to see me, Sutton. What can I do for you?" I asked politely, as though talking to a complete stranger.

He sipped his coffee. "Come on, *Christa.*" He continued to say my chosen name in a tone loaded with sarcasm. "We're not strangers. I fucked you every which way from Sunday for over a year. I know every single dip, hollow, birthmark, and ticklish spot on your entire body." He relaxed into his chair and tongued his teeth. His gaze slipped south. "I know exactly how hard to rub your clit to make you come, what your pussy tastes like, and that you've got an active gag reflex which is why you're shit at sucking cock. What's the point in playing coy?"

I swallowed past a lump of bile that blistered my throat but refused to allow him to control me, to have power over me. He'd done all those things to Sienna, not to me. She'd been the naïve one, the gullible, hopeless romantic who'd believed in fairy tales.

"You also know how I bleed. What I look like with my face battered and bruised and vile words carved into my skin. How easy it is to snap my bones." I pressed my fingers into the table and leaned forward. "But the one thing you never broke was my spirit. You threw everything at me, and yet here I am. Alive, kicking, and a permanent reminder of the evil bastard you are. I've said it before, Sutton. I don't understand what I ever did to make you hate me so much, but at least I am able to love and be loved. Whereas *you*," I laughed bitterly, "you don't know the meaning of the word."

He lounged in his seat and gave me one of those looks that used to instill terror in me. Except sitting there, I realized the words I'd just spoken were the truth. I used to think Sutton had broken me, but I was wrong. Dayton had painstakingly stitched together the tear in my soul and repaired the damage to my heart, but the strength to survive, to allow another man to get close, to find myself able to trust again was mine to celebrate. Christa wasn't Sienna. Christa was a much stronger, more astute woman of the world. I preferred her. Hell, I *loved* her.

And right then, the hold Sutton had over me disappeared as quickly as a leaf blown away by a stiff wind. He might have gained access to Max, but I knew Sutton. He'd grow bored the second he realized his actions no longer affected me. His sole reason for going after Max was to torment me, but it was almost like an animal taunting its prey. He wanted to smell the fear, to witness the torture, to know he had the potential to destroy me. Except I was taking back the power. No longer would I call myself a victim. Dayton's love and support had given me the strength and the courage to fight the man sitting opposite me.

Time to play a game of my own.

"We can sit here all day and throw insults at each other, Sutton, but what good will that do either of us? You hate me. I loathe you. But we both want the best for Max." I tried not to choke on my words. Sutton only wanted the best for one person —himself. "Right?"

His eyes flared in surprise. "Did your guard dog help you grow those claws? Because the Sienna—sorry, *Christa*—I knew wouldn't have dared to be so bold."

I crossed my legs and rested my hands in my lap, the casual devil-may-care posture carefully chosen to appear nonchalant. "You don't know me anymore, Sutton. Three years is a long time. I'm not the girl I once was."

But you're still the same guy, you vicious asshole.

"So, you're giving up fighting me on the Max thing?" He sneered. "Not that it would do you any good, but still, watching you lose your mind would have been fun."

I picked up my coffee cup and eyed him over the rim. "No, I'm not going to fight you, as long as you abide by the rules of the court." I took a sip then set down the cup. "But let me be clear about one thing. If you harm one hair on my son's head, *I will kill you.*"

Sutton smirked. "Claws indeed, little lamb. A wolf in sheep's clothing."

"I mean it, Sutton. Remember, there is nothing on Earth more protective than a lioness with her cubs. Having Max gave me a backbone. Mark my words, you hurt my son, and I will end your life—and I'll enjoy it."

His eyes narrowed, his stare direct and almost fevered. "You know, I'm getting off on this stronger side to your character. It'll make it much more enjoyable when I fucking break you. Every time I come to pick Max up, I want it to feel like a knife to your gut, and when you think you can't take the agony anymore, I'm going to twist the blade, slice your flesh, bleed you out. I'm gonna wreck you, Christa, Sienna, whatever your fucking name is this week. You think that rich fucker you've hooked up with will save you? He won't."

I could barely breathe but I held his gaze. I wouldn't give him the satisfaction of looking away, of knowing his words scared the shit out of me, despite my earlier epiphany. I gripped my coffee cup to hide the tremor of my hands. "And this is why you wanted to see me?" My words came out steady, but my throat burned raw. "Really, you could have emailed, saved us both the bother."

The faintest glimmer of a smile tugged at his lips. He twisted in his seat and dangled his right arm over the back of his chair, then crossed his ankle over his opposing knee and grazed a hand over his chin. He was trying to appear casual, unaffected by how I was standing up to him, but I knew the real Sutton. Beneath the mellow outer shell was a seething mass of rage. He'd assumed his threats would force me into submission, for my fear at his open hostility to turn me into a quivering mess, and yet I'd stood my ground and refused to bow to his will.

"You'd do well to remember something, sweetheart. Wherever you go, whatever you do, I'm watching." He downed the rest of his coffee, then got to his feet. "I'm *always* watching."

He buttoned up his jacket and met my gaze once more. His lifeless eyes locked on mine. "Rochelle hates you more than I do, if that's even possible. If I were you, I'd be more worried about what she's gonna do to you."

A dart of agony pierced my chest. Once we had been the best of friends, but blood truly was thicker than water, and when

Sutton had come after me, she'd stood shoulder to shoulder with him, his animosity toward me poisoning our friendship until I barely recognized the girl I'd once treated like a sister.

"I'm not scared of you, Sutton." I feigned a yawn. "And, frankly, Rochelle barely registers above an irritation."

A muscle in his jaw ticked, a sure sign I'd gotten to him. "I'll pick the brat up at six on Friday night. Make sure he's ready."

An ache bloomed within me at the thought of Max spending the weekend with a man who had so little regard for his well-being, but the court had made its decision, and right then, I had no weapons in my arsenal, no choice but to swallow my fear and pray to God no harm came to my son. My earlier threat had been anything but hollow. If Sutton harmed a single hair on Max's head, I'd put a bullet in his brain.

I waited for him to leave. As soon as he was out of sight, I collapsed, my shoulders sagging. I sucked in a proper breath, filling my lungs with much needed oxygen. I'd done it. I'd faced him all alone, and I'd survived.

Now, I just had to confess to Dayton.

———

"You fucking did what?"

I stood in front of Dayton, pleading with my eyes for him to calm down. I'd waited until he'd returned home from work, late because he'd been at a meeting, and then I'd hit him with it.

"Shush." I flapped my hands in a downward motion. "You'll wake Max. I didn't want to lie to you, but I needed to do it, Dayton. I had to face him by myself, let him have his five minutes of trying to scare me. But don't you see? He lost. I held my own, and he left with nothing. I didn't involve you because it's better this way. You'd have only inflamed the situation."

"Better this way?" he hissed under his breath, glowering at me, his cheeks flushed with anger. He shrugged out of his jacket and tossed it on a chair then tore off his tie. His nostrils flared as he unfastened his top button, as though his collar was strangling him. "You sat down—*alone*—for a cozy lunch with your psychopathic ex, and you think that was a good fucking idea?"

I expelled a frustrated huff. "It wasn't a cozy lunch, and I wasn't alone. It was a fifteen-minute meeting surrounded by about a hundred people." I threw my hands in the air. "By reacting this way, you're simply proving me right."

"So, because you knew I'd be furious, you lied to me instead?" He laughed bitterly. "That doesn't say much for our relationship, Christa."

I planted my hands on my hips. "Okay, let's say I had come to you and told you I was going to meet him. What would you have done?"

"I'd have forbidden it."

My eyes widened. "*Forbidden* it?" I stepped right up to him and poked him in the chest. "Let's get one thing clear, right now. You can't forbid me to do anything because you don't own me. I'll do whatever I damn well please."

If I weren't so angry, I'd take a moment to celebrate. For the second time that day, I was standing up for myself against a powerful, domineering man. Dayton might be the guy I'd fallen in love with, but that didn't mean I had to bend to his will.

"Not when it comes to him you won't. Don't you get it? I'm trying to protect you."

A red mist descended, and the muscles in my legs quivered. I locked my knees, holding firm. "Well maybe I don't need protecting!"

We stood, toe to toe, both certain we were right, neither willing to give an inch.

"Fine," Dayton spat. "Have it your way, but when you calm the fuck down and think about this, you'll know I'm right. Meeting Atwood was a dumb move. When you're ready to admit it, I'll be in my study."

He stomped across the living room and disappeared. An instant later, his study door slammed. I stuffed my hands in my hair and tugged. *Argh! Such a frustrating, stubborn ass.* And he was wrong; meeting Sutton had done me the power of good. Sure, the thought of him getting to spend time with Max instilled a fear in me so great, I could barely breathe. But I'd needed to show him that I had fire in my belly, that the weak, clingy woman who'd allowed a vicious bully to wreck her didn't exist any longer. That his threats fell on deaf ears.

I need air.

I quickly checked on Max. Fast asleep. Good. I left Dayton a note telling him I'd gone for a walk in case he came looking for me and panicked when I wasn't there. I spilled onto the street and sucked in a great lungful of humid air. By the time I'd pounded the sidewalk for a few blocks, sweat beaded at the nape of my neck. It might be past ten in the evening, but it was still very warm.

I went into a grocery store to pick up a bottle of water. I crossed to the line of coolers on the back wall, but as I opened the door, a distinct chill came over me, a feeling of being watched. Sutton's comments earlier that day came rushing back. I glanced over my shoulder, but apart from a young couple with a baby out late to pick up a few necessities, and an elderly lady giving every loaf of bread a good squeeze before finally choosing one, no one was around.

I laughed softly. *Idiot.* I grabbed the water and headed for the checkout area. After paying, I wandered back out onto the street, still crammed with tourists, and blended into the crowd. I hadn't gone very far when my skin tingled. Stopping quickly, I spun around. The guy right behind almost collided with me.

"Shit, sorry," I said.

He glared, mumbled something unintelligible, then shuffled off.

I carried on a bit farther, but when I couldn't shake the

uneasy feeling, I set off for home. I breathed a sigh of relief as my building came into view. I lengthened my stride, wanting to get inside now, to make up with Dayton and then take him to bed.

I was fifty feet from the front door when Rochelle came out of nowhere, blocking my way. Her eyes glinted with loathing.

"Not now, Rochelle," I said wearily. The last thing I needed was another altercation with an Atwood. I stepped around her, but she shifted backward, stopping me. Adrenaline pumped through my blood, my senses on high alert. The earlier prickling feeling rushed back, the sensation akin to dozens of pins piercing my skin.

"What do you want?" I asked.

Her lips curled, the smile cruel and without warmth. "Retribution," she said quietly.

I raised my eyebrows and gathered my courage. "Retribution?" I snorted. "I think you and Sutton have had your fair share on that score. I almost died, nearly lost my baby, had to move across the country leaving behind everything I'd ever known, and now, *now* I have to let my precious boy spend time with the very people who wanted him dead. The boy," I pointed at her, "your psychopathic brother tried to kill before he'd even had a chance at life. So you know what, Rochelle? You can take your retribution and shove it up your ass!"

I shifted around her once more, but she counter-moved. "You were supposed to die," she said, her voice eerily calm. "If you'd just died... Everything would have been okay."

My breath caught. *Holy fuck.* She admitted it. I desperately looked around for witnesses, anyone who might have heard her, but no one was remotely interested in the two women squaring up to each other.

"You're vile," I said. "Both you and your brother. What did I ever do to you to deserve this? We were friends."

She shrugged. "I guess you could call us friends—at first. But then you got yourself knocked up and ruined everything."

I shook my head. "I've heard enough of your deranged ramblings."

I tried to get past her for a third time. She responded by shoving me in the shoulder. I stumbled but managed to stay upright.

"You'll leave when I say you can leave."

I shivered at the sinister undertone to her voice. I'd rather she yelled, shouted, railed, pulled my hair, scratched me with her nails. I could fight her then, but this hushed, calm demeanor was much harder to deal with.

"You're just a whore, a slut from the streets, a nobody."

My thighs shook at her spiteful words, but I wasn't about to let her get away with denigrating my character. If Rochelle thought she had a chance of stripping me bare, of stealing my hard-fought confidence, I was about to disappoint her.

"Still, I took on your family and won."

Rochelle's lips clamped into a thin line, and I laughed. "You're just a replica of Sutton, Rochelle. A bully who gets their kicks out of picking on those they see as inferior." I widened my stance, letting my arms hang loose by my sides. "You want me? Come get me."

I readied myself for a slap. It was exactly the kind of thing Rochelle would do. Instead, a glimmer of a smile touched her lips. "Oh, Sienna, this must be killing you. The thought of being forced to allow your precious offspring to spend time with the very man who tried to make sure he never existed." She bent her head to the side. "Maybe my brother is right after all. Perhaps driving you crazy will be more fun than seeing you dead. You know, the more I think about it, the more I'm coming around to his way of thinking."

She'd fired an arrow and hit the bullseye. I gulped back a sob and barged her out of my way. I broke into a jog, Rochelle's wicked cackling following me.

"I can find you anytime, Sienna," she called out. "There's no hiding place. Remember that."

I almost tripped through the entranceway and sped across the lobby to our private elevator. Only once inside did I allow myself to breathe, but as I took a lungful of air, my legs gave way, and I sank down the wall.

The elevator doors glided open. I sat there for a few seconds, wondering if my legs would support me. I'd never been the kind of person who took well to conflict, and yet today, I'd had to face three separate battles: Sutton, Dayton, and now Rochelle.

The doors began to close. I struggled to my feet and stuck my arm through the diminishing gap. They sprang open once more. My thigh muscles quivered with a combination of fear and rapidly dwindling anger. As I walked into the living room, I found Dayton pacing, my note in his hand.

"Where the fuck have you been?" he bit out, his high cheekbones reddened with anger.

I let my purse fall to the floor and, as the stress of the day came crashing down, I burst into tears.

"Jesus, Christa." He closed the gap between us and cupped my face. "Angel, what's wrong? Are you hurt? What's happened?"

I wrapped my arms around his waist and buried my head in his chest. "Hold me, please," I choked out.

Dayton rubbed the palm of his hand over my back. "Always, angel. Always. But please, tell me you're not hurt."

I shook my head. I wasn't, not physically anyway, but for some strange reason, Rochelle's nasty outburst had affected me far more than Sutton's attempts at intimidation that afternoon. I'd stood up to him, and to Dayton. So why hadn't I done the same to Rochelle? I should have slapped her, scored my nails down her too-perfect face, kicked her ass right into the street. Except I wasn't a violent person—I hated violence of any kind—and Rochelle had once been my friend. That was what hurt the most. I'd lost someone I'd once considered as close as the sister I hadn't been blessed with.

After a minute or so, I collected myself. I dried my tears, then met Dayton's worried gaze.

"I bumped into Rochelle," I said.

His eyes opened wide. "She spoke to you?"

I nodded. "If you can call it that."

His jaw clenched tight. "What did she say?"

I shrugged. "It doesn't matter." When he opened his mouth, probably to disagree and tell me that it did matter, I added, "She did say an odd thing, though. That she could find me anytime, and I should remember that." Sutton's earlier comment nudged at me. "And today, Sutton told me he was always watching. Do you think they're following me? Is that why I'm getting these creepy sensations of being spied on all the time?"

Dayton squeezed my arm. "Neither of them will hurt you, I promise." And then he narrowed his gaze. "Where's your phone?"

"In my purse, why?"

"Give it to me."

I bent down, retrieved it from my bag, and handed it to him. Without saying another word, Dayton strode in the direction of his study. I followed. By the time I arrived, he already had my phone hooked up to his computer.

"What's the matter?" I asked.

He shook his head but didn't answer me. I perched on the end of his desk, waiting as he bashed furiously on his keyboard. A couple of minutes later, he muttered, "Son of a bitch."

"What? Dayton you're scaring me. What's going on?"

He lifted his head. "Your phone has been tapped. Not only does this mean Atwood can hear every phone call you make, but it also means he can trace where you are day or night, as long as you have your phone with you, of course."

My lips parted in shock. "W-what? How?"

He twisted his lips wryly. "Lots of ways, mostly illegal." He picked up my phone and stared at it. "Do you ever leave this out of your sight?"

"No. I mean, yeah, I guess. Sometimes. It's hard to remember. Can you get rid of it?"

"Already done. Look, I want to put a trace of my own on here, if you're in agreement."

I dampened my lips. "You mean so you'll always know where I am?"

"No. So I'll know where your phone is." He sighed, scraping a hand through his hair. "This isn't some weird attempt to keep tabs on you, Christa. But this fucker has overstepped the mark, and it's important we stay one step ahead. I also want to add some software in the background that will alert me if your phone is tampered with, or if anyone tries to install a non-standard application either physically or remotely."

I nibbled my lip, then nodded. When had my life become so complicated? I felt as if I was in the middle of a bad spy movie. "Whatever you think is best," I said. "Shouldn't we call the police? Tell them what you've found?"

He shook his head. "Without proof there's very little they can do, and all that will achieve is pissing him off. He'll soon find out we've discovered his tap when it all goes quiet at his end. I'll mention it to Francesca, though, just so she's got the full picture."

"Okay."

He cupped his hand around the back of my neck and pulled me in for a kiss. "I know you're scared, but I'm here. I won't let anything happen to you. I'm annoyed at myself for not expecting this and putting in counter measures earlier."

"You anticipated he'd do something like this?" I swept a hand over my face. "Jesus."

"I'm not surprised he's stooped this low, no. I wouldn't put anything past that fucker. Tomorrow, I want you to close down every personal email account, because he could also be hacking into those. I'll get the team at work to set you up with one you can use for personal stuff, but it'll go through our firewalls, making it far more secure. Web-based email is easy to hack into, if you know what you're doing."

God, this was all too much information. Too much to take in and deal with in one hit. Swamped with acute exhaustion, I rose from Dayton's desk. "I'm going to check on Max, then go to bed."

Dayton stood to kiss me. "I'll finish up here and be in shortly. Try not to worry."

I closed the door to his study. *Try not to worry? Impossible.*

11

DAYTON

I LISTENED CAREFULLY until I heard the door to our bedroom click shut. I peered into the hallway just to make sure she wasn't there. Satisfied the coast was clear, I reentered my study and picked up her phone. Turning it over in my hands, I wondered how Atwood had gained access. It was far from impossible, although you had to know what you were doing. There could be a mole in the camp, although I doubted it. My company carried out detailed checks on every employee. Still, it wouldn't hurt to get my Head of Cyber Security to investigate.

I emailed him asking him to do just that, as well as instructing him to arrange for a secure personal email address to be set up for Christa. My next call was to Draven.

"Hey, Dayton. What's up?"

"Found anything worthwhile yet?"

Draven barked out a booming laugh. "Not yet. These things take time, brother. I had one case that took me six months to crack. Hang in there. If there's shit to find, I'll find it."

"I hope so." I was a man who measured by results, not promises. "That's not the main reason I'm calling, though."

"Oh yeah?"

"I need someone who can provide round-the-clock surveillance on two, no, make that three, people. Cole told me that was part of your repertoire. Can you arrange it?"

Draven whistled through his teeth. "That's gonna cost. For how long?"

"As long as it takes."

"Maybe I'll be able to afford that shack in the Bahamas after all."

I laughed. I seriously liked this guy. "Do this right, and you'll be able to afford a plantation house."

"I take it Atwood is one of the targets?"

I nodded even though he couldn't see me. "Plus his sister, Rochelle, and Atwood's dog, Kawalski."

"The guy you bloodied up?"

"The very same."

"Any intervention, or straight-up surveillance?"

"Straight-up, unless Christa or Max is involved, and then it has to appear as if it's a random act of kindness by a stranger. I don't want your cover blown, unless either of them is in physical danger, which I doubt. Atwood isn't that stupid."

"Got it." He told me his fee.

I didn't even flinch.

"The courts gave him weekend access to Max," I shared. "I want extra eyes on whenever Atwood has him."

"Understood."

"He's picking him up this Friday and won't return him until Sunday. I want hourly reports regarding Max's welfare."

"You want my team to start Friday?"

"No," I replied. "I want them to start now."

———

Christa held it together when Atwood came for Max that Friday. I didn't know whether to be relieved or pissed when Max happily went with him, his little backpack hoisted on his shoulders, and his favorite toy dangling from one hand. I didn't want Max to suffer, but at the same time, jealousy carved a fucking great hole in my stomach at the thought of Max getting close to that bastard. For all intents and purposes, he was *my* kid. I loved him in a way Atwood wasn't capable of.

Once the elevator doors closed, Christa walked stiffly past me and back into the penthouse. "Drink?" she asked, heading for the fridge. She held a bottle of wine in the air. "Because I need one."

"Sure." I flopped onto the couch and pinched the bridge of my nose between my thumb and forefinger.

She came over with our drinks and sat beside me. "What if he doesn't take care of him?" she asked. "I mean, I know my fears are probably unfounded. Sutton's a smart guy, and he'd know that if any harm comes to Max, his leverage is over, but still, I can't help worrying. He's my baby."

I'd kept hiring Draven from Christa so far, with good intentions. I hadn't wanted to put the fear of God into her that I felt it necessary to have Atwood, his sister, and his sidekick followed twenty-four seven. But the more I thought about it, the more peace it brought me. We had someone on our side, watching over Max when we couldn't. Draven had even assured me that they had eyes and ears inside the hotel room Atwood was renting while he searched for a more permanent residence. I didn't know how Draven had managed that—and I didn't want to know—but regardless, it made me feel a whole lot better.

I rested an arm around her shoulder. "Max will be fine. I've got someone watching him."

She straightened, her eyes opened wide. "What do you mean, someone watching him?"

I grazed a hand over my chin, uncertain how she'd take this. "A cop I know put me in touch with a guy who runs an investigative and private security firm." I shrugged. "I hired him and his team to follow Atwood, his sister, and Kawalski. On the days Atwood has Max, there's extra security, and they're going to send regular reports, so we know what's happening."

She covered her mouth with her hand, her eyes darting left and right. And then she straddled my legs and hugged me so tight I couldn't breathe. "Oh God, Dayton. Thank you. Thank you. You don't know how worried I've been." She kissed me hard on the lips, then straightened. "He's good, this guy?"

"Apparently, he's the best." I grinned. "I wasn't sure how you'd take it. I don't think his methods are entirely legal. He told me he's got eyes and ears inside the hotel room Atwood is staying in."

"I don't care if it's not legal," she said firmly. "Sutton won't play by the rules, so we can't either. We need to do everything we can to stay one step ahead."

My thoughts entirely.

I tucked her hair behind her ears. "I was thinking of taking you somewhere tomorrow and staying overnight. We'll be back in plenty of time for Max coming home on Sunday. It'll do us good to get away for a little while. Hanging around this place all weekend won't be fun for either of us."

She curled her lips to the side, considering. "What if we need to hurry back?"

I'd expected this argument and I'd prepared for it. "We can be home in less than two hours."

"Oh, Dayton, that's too far. What if Max needs me?"

I cupped her cheek. "Angel, we've got eyes on him, twenty-four seven. Draven's team knows to move in immediately if they think that Max is in any danger. Look, you know as well as I do that Atwood won't hurt him. We know what Atwood's agenda is. Max is simply the vehicle to exact his revenge, his weapon of choice, if you will."

She winced, tugging on her bottom lip as she mulled over my

argument, her gaze somewhere over my left shoulder. And then she nodded.

"Okay. I guess it will be good to get away. I can't bear the thought of being here without Max." Her voice broke, and her eyes filled with tears. She dashed at them with the back of her hand. "Sorry. I promised myself I wouldn't cry."

I drew my knuckles down her damp cheek. "You don't have to pretend to me that this isn't killing you. It's killing me, too."

She fisted her hands in my shirt and tugged me forward, then pressed her lips to mine. "I love you so goddamn much, Dayton Somers. I couldn't do this alone."

"Yes, you could," I said. "But I'm glad you don't have to."

"God, me, too." She grinned. "So where are you taking me for our dirty weekend away?"

I tapped the side of my nose. "You'll have to wait and see."

12

CHRISTA

I SHOULD HAVE EXPECTED a man as rich as Dayton to have his own plane but, truth be told, it hadn't occurred to me, and because he'd driven on the trips we'd taken to the Cape and up to the Catskills, there hadn't been a need for me to know.

Well, I knew now, but still, the sheer luxury of the interior blew me away. Soft, gray leather seating, thick, carpeted flooring, light-ash wood paneling. There was even a three-seater couch along one side, and opposite, a large flat-panel TV. *Holy crap.*

"Wow," I said, because it was the only word that came to mind. I puffed up my cheeks, blowing the air out slowly. "This is…" I blinked. "Wow."

Dayton chuckled. "I'd have brought you onboard before, but the right time never arose, until now." He touched my elbow, guiding me to one of the plush high-backed chairs, then sat opposite. "Buckle up. We'll be taking off in a few minutes."

Doubt at leaving Max behind nudged me once more. The argument Dayton had used on me last night was a solid one, but that didn't stop me worrying.

"What if Draven or his team need to contact us while we're in the air?"

Dayton reached across the table separating us and knitted our fingers together. "We have WiFi onboard. Any problems, and I'll have the plane turned around immediately. Angel, try to relax. I know it's hard, but you need this break. Trust me, please."

His earnest expression won me over. Dayton had done everything within his power to secure Max's safety and my peace of mind. The only thing that would make things any better was tomorrow evening when Max was returned to me. In the meantime, Dayton was doing his very best to distract me, and I loved him for it.

"You're very persuasive."

He chuckled. "It's part of my charm."

The plane sped down the runway, easing smoothly into the air. The cloudless sky made our ascent turbulence free, and twenty minutes later, we leveled off. I'd only taken one flight in my life before—the one that had brought me to New York from Seattle—but the experiences were incomparable. Flying coach was about as much fun as having your teeth drilled, but this... God, I didn't want it to end.

When the plane touched down, I peered out of the window, but there weren't any clues as to where we'd landed. Dayton had been true to his word; the flight had taken us about ninety minutes door-to-door.

"Are you going to tell me where we are yet?"

"Canada," he replied.

"Canada!" I squeaked.

Dayton unbuckled his belt and stood. He reached into his inside pocket and pulled out my passport—the one he'd insisted I get a few weeks ago 'just in case.'

"You little sneak. How long have you been planning this?" I asked, narrowing my gaze.

I expected him to laugh at my teasing. Instead, his mouth

turned down at the edges. "I'd planned to take you and Max abroad this summer. To Europe, actually." He shrugged, disappointment obvious in the hunch of his shoulders. "Still, there's always next summer."

Providing the judge has decreed I can take Max out of the country by then.

I released my seat belt and rose from my chair. I wrapped my arms around his waist and looked up at him.

"You don't have to take me to fancy places. I just want to be with you."

He captured a lock of my hair, feeding it through his fingers. "I know. It's one of the things I love about you. You're not interested in my money."

"No." I trailed my hand over his chest, his abdomen, then reached between his legs and cupped his junk. "But I am interested in your cock."

He threw back his head and laughed, growing hard in my hand. "I knew there had to be a reason you'd stuck around."

I grinned, glad to have erased the sadness. I didn't like it when Dayton was unhappy, and I'd seen too much of it lately. "You're lucky it's big and you know what to do with it, otherwise…" I hitched a shoulder. "It'd be *sayonara.*"

He arched an eyebrow. "Is that so?"

"Yup," I said.

He curved his hands underneath my ass, then hoisted my legs around his waist. He tilted his hips, rubbing his erection right where he knew it'd make me gasp. I moved in for a kiss, but the plane door opening interrupted my plans. Embarrassed to have been caught in such a compromising position, I wriggled until Dayton had no choice but to put me down. Heat rushed into my cheeks as an official-looking man averted his gaze.

"Mr. Somers," he said, clearing his throat. "We've been expecting you. May I see your passports?"

Dayton turned his head, displeasure at the untimely interruption drawing his brows into a deep frown. "Wait outside," he snapped.

The guy turned beet-red, muttered an apology, and disappeared through the doorway.

"Dayton," I admonished, giving him my best glare. Honestly, sometimes it was like he showed one side of himself to me and a completely different side to everyone else.

He lifted me back into position, ignoring my reprimand. "Now," he murmured. "Where were we?"

His tongue slid between my lips, parting them. He took control of the kiss, devouring me, making me forget that I was apart from my son, if only for a few seconds. He drew back, a wicked expression on his face. "On the return journey, get ready to join the mile-high club, Ms. Adams."

I grinned as he put me down. "Sir, yes, sir." I mock saluted him.

He nipped at my lower lip. "You can call me that later, when I'm buried inside you."

I snorted. "In your dreams."

He bent his head low, his mouth inches from mine. "I like a challenge."

"There's an achievable goal, and then there's an impossible goal."

He laughed and took my hand. "Shall we go?"

He didn't wait for an answer before heading down the metal staircase. The airport official was waiting at the bottom, head bent, like a child who had been sent to wait outside the principle's office. Without a word, Dayton handed over our passports. The guy did his official bit, handed them back, muttered, "Welcome to Canada," and trotted off in the direction of a low-lying white building.

"I think you might be off his Christmas card list," I said to Dayton who responded with a roll of his eyes.

"Come on, the car's waiting."

We got into a black limo and, as soon as we were buckled into our seats, the car pulled smoothly away.

"Any word on Max?" I asked.

Dayton had been in touch with Draven regularly since Sutton had picked him up last night around six, and so far, the news coming back was that Max was fine, settled, and happy. I knew Draven's intel came from illegal sources, but I didn't care. The only thing on my mind was Max's welfare. Screw the law. It sure had screwed me.

Dayton took out his phone and stared at it, occasionally tapping his finger against the screen. "Max is fine. Atwood has hired a nanny to help. Draven's checked her out, and she's legit."

I breathed out a sigh of relief, the same breath I'd exhaled every time Draven had been in contact. I was counting the hours until Max was back in my care, but as I caught Dayton's concerned expression, the slight downward turn to his mouth, the frown lines between his brows, I forced myself to perk up. Dayton was worried enough, about me, about Max, I didn't want to ruin this short trip for him, or for me. I needed the break as much as he did, and I knew, deep down, Max was perfectly safe. Sutton was a lot of things, but he wasn't stupid enough to bring any harm to Max. Still, the round the clock security did offer an additional sense of reassurance.

"So, what're your plans, Somers?"

He captured my hand and brought it to his lips, pressing a soft kiss to my knuckles. "Have you ever seen Niagara Falls up close?"

My mouth popped open. "You know I haven't." I broke into a smile. "That's what we're doing?" I gripped his arm and gave it an excited shake. "That's what we're doing!" I repeated.

He laughed. "Yes."

I clapped my hands to my cheeks. "Oh my God." And then a thought occurred to me, one that took the edge off my excitement. "Have you been before?"

"Not like this," he said. "I've flown over in a plane, but that's it. We're going to see them from the water, from behind the falls, and from the air in a helicopter."

I blinked rapidly as my eyes misted over. "This is just what I needed." My voice broke, and I cleared my throat.

He caressed my arm. "I know," he said softly.

And right there, in those two quiet words, was the reason why I loved this man so deeply. I didn't have to explain myself for Dayton to understand my needs, to know what would bring me comfort. He got me... instinctively and completely.

We arrived at the hotel where we'd spend that night, dropped off our things, and immediately headed out. Dayton explained we'd be doing the boat ride first, which would take us to the very edge of the Horseshoe Falls. I buzzed with excitement as he helped me aboard. We were handed a poncho each. The second Dayton slipped his over his head, I burst out laughing.

"If your employees could see you now," I teased, pretending to reach for my phone to snap a picture.

He grabbed my wrist and waggled his finger in front of my face. "Don't even think about it."

As the boat headed out, we received word from Draven that Sutton, Rochelle, and the nanny were at Brooklyn Bridge Park with Max. Draven had sent some pictures that I pored over. Max looked happy, his cheeks rosy, his eyes bright, his smile broad. On the one hand, seeing Max enjoying himself warmed my heart; I wanted my son to remain unaware of the intense battle being fought over him. On the other hand, I was pissed because that park had been on my list of places to take him this summer. Still, at least Sutton had taken Max somewhere, rather than keep him cooped up in a hotel room all weekend. It was far too nice to stay indoors.

"You okay?" Dayton curved an arm around my shoulder, pulling me close.

I nodded and painted on a bright smile. "He seems to be having a great time."

His mouth creased in thought. "I wish he was here with us."

I stood on tiptoes and kissed his cheek. "Me, too."

Our despondency over Max eased a little as we closed in on the magnificent waterfall. I'd seen Niagara Falls on the TV, of course, but up close was a different experience entirely. The sound of the cascading water almost deafened me, and spray soaked me in seconds. But, God, I wouldn't have missed it for the world.

I tried to shout to Dayton, but there was no chance of being heard, so I simply snuggled against him, wrapped his arms around my middle, and fixed my attention on the amazing, natural wonder.

I'd thought nothing could beat the view of millions of gallons of water crashing down from over one hundred and seventy feet above me. Turned out I was wrong. The 'Journey behind the Falls' allowed us to explore the scenic tunnels and get a different view of the gushing waterfall, and the helicopter ride where we not only flew over Horseshoe Falls, but also Bridal Veil Falls literally sucked the breath from my lungs. How small humans were when compared with the magnificence of nature.

We returned to the hotel later that day, tired but exhilarated. I could hardly believe we'd only flown into Canada that morning. It felt so long ago since we were on Dayton's plane, but as great as the day had been, I was also looking forward to flying home again tomorrow—because I'd be returning to Max. Sutton was due to bring him back by six, and I couldn't wait.

"I'm going to take a bath before dinner," I said, stretching my back out. "I ache all over."

Dayton caught my hips and pulled me closer. "Room for two?" he asked.

"Not a chance," I said. "A bath is something to be enjoyed alone."

"And here I was thinking you loved me." He released me to reach inside his jacket pocket and remove his phone as a text came in. He glanced at the screen, frowned, then turned his attention back to me. "I need to make a quick call."

"Is it about Max?" I asked, my breath hitching.

He shook his head. "It's work, that's all. Why don't you go take your bath and I'll be in to scrub your back shortly."

I grinned. "Okay, but remember all work and no play makes Dayton a very dull boy indeed."

He took a swipe at my ass, but I skipped out of his way and headed into the bathroom, laughing. *I hope that call is a quick one.*

13

DAYTON

I ANSWERED MY PHONE. "Hold on a second." I waited for the bathroom door to click shut and the sound of running water to reach me. "This had better not be a social call."

Draven's low chuckle came at me down the line. "It is, actually. I thought you might wanna go for a beer rather than bang your woman."

I laughed. Draven already seemed to know the right thing to say to take the edge off when I was irritated. "Fuck off. What's the real reason?"

"I need you to come to Seattle."

I rolled my neck from side to side, easing out the kinks. "Why?"

"I may have something."

"Define something." Interest spiked my heartrate, and I began to pace.

"Suffice to say it's got the potential to be explosive. You asked for dirt. I think I've found a fucking mud pit. There's someone you need to meet."

My heart didn't just beat faster with that news. It galloped, thumping against my ribcage. "I can be there Monday. Can it wait until then?" I had no idea how I'd explain to Christa if Draven needed me there immediately, but I'd think of something.

"It'll wait."

"Good. I'll text you when I know what time I'll be there."

I cut the call and tossed my phone onto the bed. I fucking *knew* it. I might not know what Draven had yet, but there was no way he'd drag me all the way across the country for scraps. No, whatever he'd found could be the answer I'd been hoping for.

The sound of running water coming from the bathroom stopped. I crossed the room and opened the door. Christa was already in the bath, a towel behind her head, bubbles up to her neck.

"Everything okay?" she asked, eyes closed.

I reached over her and picked up a sponge. Perching on the edge of the bath, I dipped it in the hot water then squeezed it over her chest. The bubbles parted, giving me a perfect glimpse of her breasts.

"It's fine," I said, repeating the action. My cock stirred to life. "But I do have to fly to the west coast first thing Monday." I purposely avoided mentioning the city. I didn't want her to make any connection to Atwood.

"Make sure you bring me back some Ghirardelli chocolate," she said, misinterpreting my destination as San Francisco, as I'd hoped.

"Would I dare return without it?" I asked, making a mental note to pick some up before my return journey.

"No." She giggled. "You know me so well."

I palmed her breast, brushing my thumb over her nipple. It pebbled under my touch. She gave a soft sigh and thrust her chest forward. I knelt beside the bath and leaned over, pulling her erect nipple into my mouth. I sucked hard, then released her. "Still only room for one?" I asked.

"Get in here," she growled.

I chuckled. Stripping off my clothes, I tossed them to one

side. She shuffled forward, making room for me to get in behind her. I slid my legs either side of her. My now fully erect cock settled between her ass cheeks. I brushed her damp hair over her shoulder and traced the tip of my tongue over the nape of her neck.

Squeezing a dollop of bodywash into my palm, I rubbed my hands together. "Do you know how sexy you are, all wet and soapy," I said, because it wasn't a question. It was a statement of fact.

She murmured but didn't respond. I hadn't expected her to.

I rubbed the suds over her shoulder blades, then moved down to her breasts. She placed her hands over the top of mine as I bathed her, tracing my movements. I inched beneath the water line, my palm flat against her abdomen. I continued farther down, cupping her mound. She raised her knees and parted her thighs, and I slipped my hand between them, then slid a finger between her folds. She let out a breath of air.

"That feels so good. More like that, please."

I grinned, adding a second finger. I circled her clit with my thumb and nibbled her shoulder. "Want to join in?" I asked, a slight hesitation to my tone. I wasn't sure how she'd take my request but, hell, the idea of her fingers and mine inside her made me so fucking hard.

For a few seconds she froze. And then, tentatively, she slid her middle finger inside herself.

"That feels weird," she said.

"I'm not forcing you to do anything you don't want to."

"Oh no. I didn't mean bad weird. I meant good weird."

I cupped her chin with my free hand and eased her head around so I could kiss her. As our tongues entwined, I upped the pace of my fingers inside her. She matched my movements, her breathing escalating the faster I went. She moaned into my mouth, and fuck, the sound tightened my balls. At this rate, I was gonna come without any direct stimulation.

I circled my hips, and my dick got the contact it craved, sliding between the crease of her ass. She wriggled against me. Water sloshed over the top of the bath, soaking the floor. I strummed her clit, and she came, her muscles pulsing around my fingers, and hers.

Gasping, she tore her mouth from mine. "Fuck, Dayton."

A rare curse spilling from her lips was enough to send me over the edge. I orgasmed, groaning, my cum mingling with the water and the bubbles, and the soft skin of her ass. I squeezed my eyes closed, my lips parting, and let out a shuddering breath.

Gulping air into my lungs, I waited for my heartbeat to slow. I tightened my arms around her and kissed her damp hair.

"Well, that was new," she said, reaching behind to caress my cheek.

"Good new?"

She twisted her head and captured my lips once more. "Amazing new."

We stayed in the bath until the water cooled. I got out first, threw a towel on the floor to mop up the excess water, then helped her out.

"Can we check on Max?"

I'd known I wouldn't be able to distract her for long, but my chest swelled with pride because I'd managed to give her a few minutes of peace, of pleasure. "Of course, angel. Let's dry you off first."

I wrapped her in a white fluffy towel. After tying one around my waist, I picked up a third and dried her arms, her legs, her feet.

"I feel so cherished," she said, using my arm to maintain her balance.

I curved a hand around her neck and kissed the top of her head. "That's because you are."

I left her drying her hair and went to fetch her nightwear. I slipped it over her head, pulled on a pair of boxers, and turned down the bed. We got in and I picked up my phone. I opened the secure app that Draven and I were communicating through, entered the password, then read out the reports he'd been sending every hour.

When I finished, Christa sighed and snuggled into my side. "At least he's okay, and he'll be home tomorrow."

"He will," I said, turning out the light.

And if Draven's news is as explosive as he suggested, maybe this'll be the first and last time Max has to spend a weekend with that fucking lunatic.

Max returned home full of excitement about his weekend away. I listened to his enthusiastic chatter as Atwood gave me his smug *I've won* expression. If the stakes weren't so high, I'd release my pent-up anger and give the fucker a beating he wouldn't forget in a hurry.

"I'll see you Wednesday, Max," Atwood said with about as much sincerity as a politician trying to persuade the voting public that they gave a shit. "And I'll see you, of course, *Christa.*"

"Actually, you won't see Christa this week," I said, squeezing her hand in warning. I'd made the decision on the fly. I knew she hated facing Atwood, and he reveled in the fact. He loved to needle her, and she deserved a break from having to face him. "But don't worry. I'll be here." I gave him my best cold stare.

Atwood turned to Christa with a vindictive glare. "I deal with you, not *him.*"

I crouched to Max's level. "Go with Mommy, Max. I'll be in shortly."

Christa shot me a grateful look and swept Max up into her arms. He rested his head on her shoulder and played with her hair. "Come on, little man. Let's get you something to eat, then bed."

I waited until I heard the click of the door behind me, and then I took a menacing step in Atwood's direction. He stood his ground, arms hanging loose by his sides as though ready for a fight. I'd give anything, *anything*, to goad him into taking a swing. I'd have an excuse, then, to kick the living shit out of him.

I straightened my spine and narrowed my gaze. "From now on, you'll be dealing with me, not Christa."

He squared up to me. "No I fucking won't."

His intense stare never wavered. Then again, neither did mine. "Yes. You will. You'll also notice that your pathetic attempt to keep tabs on her failed spectacularly." I curled my lip, sneering. "You think you're so fucking clever, but you're no match for me. Every step you take, I'll be two ahead. Every time you think you've gained an advantage, I'll tear it down. Just when you think you've won, I'm going to bring a fucking nightmare right to your door."

Atwood's cocky expression faltered, only for a second, but that was enough for me to know he wasn't nearly as sure of himself as he pretended to be.

He laughed mirthlessly. "You just made this much more interesting, Somers. Now I have two people to finish. You *and* her."

I inched closer, glaring. "We both know you haven't got the balls to take me on." I looked him up and down disparagingly. "But you're welcome to try."

Atwood put his face right in mine, close enough that I could smell his breath and a faint whiff of aftershave. He breathed noisily through his nose. "Be careful, Somers. You have no idea what I'm capable of."

I snorted. "I'm the wrong fucking sex for you to come at me. You're a nothing, a nobody, a bully who gets his kicks from scaring women. Except this time, *buddy,* you've chosen the wrong person to go into battle with." I jabbed him in the shoulder. "Now get the fuck out of my home."

I spun on my heel and went back inside, slamming the door behind me.

14

DAYTON

MY PLANE LANDED ON A DAMP, miserable morning in Seattle, but I had high hopes the day would get brighter as soon as Draven told me what he'd discovered. I walked down the steps and headed straight for the terminal building. I'd flown into a small private airfield south of the city and asked Draven to meet me there. That way, I could listen to what he had to say, come up with a plan of action, and be heading back to New York within the hour. I didn't like leaving Christa for too long, even though she'd be at the office today. I wanted to be home well before nightfall.

Draven was waiting inside the building. We shook hands, and I cocked my head, indicating for him to follow me. I led him through to an office I'd reserved where we could speak in private.

"Well, what have you got?" I asked before the guy had even sat down. I didn't have time for niceties. "It'd better be good, considering you've dragged me across the fucking country on a goddamn Monday morning."

He looked me directly in the eyes and grinned. "Nice to see

you, too, dickhead. Jesus, you talk to your woman with that mouth?"

Despite the seriousness of the situation, I smiled. "Anyone else dared to speak to me like that and I'd rip them a new asshole."

Draven chuckled. "You could try. You'd fail, but still..." He hitched a shoulder, then waggled his eyebrows.

A laugh burst from deep within me. I seriously liked this guy. When all this was over, I genuinely hoped we'd stay in touch.

He laid a folder on the desk and opened it, revealing page after page of scrawl. At the back, attached with a paperclip, was a photograph of a redheaded woman I'd guess was in her late twenties to early thirties. Draven removed it and then slid the picture across the table.

"This is Kathy Johnson. She's a thirty-one-year-old waitress and mother to a seven-year-old daughter, Tilly. She's unmarried and lives in a studio apartment on the edge of the city."

Already bored, I gave him a blank stare. "And?"

Draven smiled. Even though we barely knew each other, he appreciated my lack of patience. "I'm getting to the point, asshole. Bear with me."

I bit back a sigh and gestured for him to continue.

"When Kathy was eighteen, she waited tables in a private members club. This club was frequented by Atwood's father, and by Atwood himself when he turned twenty-one. Atwood Jr. took a liking to Miss Johnson, and would often grope her inappropriately. A pinch of her ass here, a squeeze of a tit there. She complained to the manager, but he told her to either put up with it or leave."

"Delightful," I said sarcastically, leaning forward in my seat, my interest piqued as to the direction this was heading.

"Yep," Draven said, wearing his loathing as openly as my own. "A total douche. Anyway, one night, Miss Johnson was working late and, as she left the club, Atwood approached her.

He tried to kiss her, but she was having none of it. She told him that neither he nor his money interested her, and she wasn't for sale.

"She remembers his laughter following her down the street. He called after her, telling her he liked the ones who fought back. That they turned him on the most, made him hard. It was at that point she started running. Atwood sprinted after her. Then he caught her."

Oh fuck. I knew what was coming and, despite not wanting to hear what he had to say, I nodded for him to keep going.

"He dragged her down an alleyway and raped her." Draven's face twisted. "Sounds civilized, doesn't it? Rape, sexual assault. Words we hear in the press or on the news every single day and barely bat an eye. Banal sayings that don't begin to describe the horror behind them, or the horrendous suffering the victim goes through. The truth is that Atwood raped, sodomized, and beat Kathy Johnson, then left her lying in a pool of her own blood."

I pinched the bridge of my nose as images raged through my mind, the kind no one wanted to have flash before them.

"What happened then?" I didn't want to know, yet I *had* to know. I wanted the full, disgusting truth of just what a piece of shit I was dealing with—that *Christa* was having to deal with.

"She was found by a passerby the next morning." He closed his eyes briefly. "She lay there all night in that alley, half naked, battered and bruised. The good Samaritan took her to the hospital. The police came, and she made a statement."

My ears perked up, and hope surged within me. "This is on record?"

"Yep, but don't get too excited. Before the police could bring charges, Miss Johnson recanted her statement."

"Why?" I asked and then shook my head in understanding. "They got to her."

He nodded. "Atwood sent one of his minions after her who made it very clear that if she didn't withdraw her statement, what happened to her was just the beginning. He told her that no one would believe a slut like her over an Atwood anyway, and it would be easy for them to make out that she was mentally unstable."

"Fuckers," I gritted out.

"Yeah, and it gets worse. When she had her daughter, a huge bouquet of flowers arrived at the hospital. The note read 'Stay sane – love Sutton.' She knew then that he was still watching her in case she ever revealed what happened. That message put an end to any thoughts of reporting him, because now she didn't only have herself to worry about, but a kid, too."

"Yet she told you?"

"Believe me, it wasn't easy, and if I'd still been a cop, I'd have had no chance of getting her to open up. At first she wouldn't have anything to do with me, but I persisted. I think because I believed her about Atwood and what he was capable of." He shrugged. "Well, in the end, she caved. It must have been a helluva relief to share such a fucking big skeleton."

Elated, I said, "She's willing to press charges now?"

"Ah, not exactly. That's what I wanted to talk to you about. She won't go to the police. She's terrified that if her mental health is brought into question—and let's face it, Atwood has the means to pay the right psychiatrists to say whatever the fuck he wants—she could lose her daughter. She won't admit, formally, that she ever knew Sutton Atwood or his piece-of-shit father who allowed the brutal assault of a young girl to be covered up to save his precious son's ass."

"Fuck." I scraped a hand over my face, my mind racing. "There must be something we can do to persuade her. What if I could convince her that I'd protect her, and her kid?"

Draven stroked his beard. "Worth a try, I guess."

I picked up the photo of the girl and stared at it. "Set it up."

———

I called Christa, informing her something had come up that needed my immediate attention and I'd be home tomorrow. I made her promise not to leave the penthouse after Paul took her home after work. Her rapid reassurance calmed me.

Angie booked me in at the Four Seasons and arranged for a change of clothes to be sent over. Draven dropped me off at the hotel, promising to return later. I spent the day working, but my mind wasn't on the job. All I could think was that if everything worked out, Atwood could soon be eating his meals off a plastic tray and taking a shit in public.

At eight that evening, I went down to the lobby to find Draven already waiting. We'd arranged to meet Miss Johnson in a bar on the other side of town.

"What's she like?" I asked him as he filtered into the traffic. I needed to know what I was dealing with so I could plan accordingly.

"She's what I'd call a 'nice girl.' Definitely not the type who has the chops to deal with a clever, manipulative bastard like Atwood. She's also skittish as shit, unsurprisingly."

I nodded, then stared out of the window, planning my approach, while Draven turned up the radio. We arrived at the bar a few minutes early. Inside, it was dark and dingy, and definitely not my kind of establishment, but that also made it a good meeting place because if this wasn't the type of bar I visited, it wasn't Atwood's either.

I slipped into a booth, Draven taking a seat opposite, and called over the bartender. Draven ordered a whiskey, I stuck to coffee. I wanted to keep my wits about me.

Fifteen minutes later, we were still sitting there, no sign of Kathy. I ordered another round of drinks.

"She gonna bail?" I asked, and then I saw her. "Forget it, she's here."

I got to my feet. She saw me, hesitated, and then walked in my direction on wobbly legs. One look at her told me I had to treat this one very gently. When Draven had said "skittish" he wasn't wrong. Highly fucking strung was a better description. Her knuckles were almost white where they gripped the strap of her purse, and she kept looking over her shoulder as if expecting Atwood to appear at any moment.

"Miss Johnson." I stuck out my hand. "I'm Dayton Somers. Thank you for meeting with me." We shook, her small, cold hand getting lost in my much larger one. "You remember Draven."

She nodded, then slid onto the seat opposite, next to Draven. She was far too skinny, but as I ran my gaze over her, I couldn't see any needle marks. I wouldn't have blamed her if she'd chosen to bury her fear in addiction, although I was grateful for her kid that she'd decided on a different path.

"Would you like a drink?" I asked gently, conscious that I could sometimes come over as a little overbearing, and I didn't want her bolting before we'd had a chance to talk. Although compared with how Draven looked, I was a teddy bear.

She nibbled her lip. "Water, please. I don't drink, and coffee makes me sick."

Another tick in her favor. No drugs. No alcohol. It would make her an excellent witness—if I could persuade her to go to the cops.

I waited until she had a glass of iced water in front of her and she'd taken a couple of tentative sips. "Miss Johnson, I'm going to cut to the chase. Draven has updated me on what happened to you, and I'd like to start by saying that I am terribly sorry for what you went through."

She kept her attention on the table. "Thank you."

"What you're not aware of is that my girlfriend went through something similar. Not exactly the same. She wasn't raped." I winced. "But she was severely beaten and mutilated and she almost lost a child." Miss Johnson's head snapped up, but I continued. "The difference between you and my girlfriend is that

Atwood is the father of her baby. And on this occasion, he got another man to carry out the attack, rather than getting his own hands dirty."

Her eyes welled up, and she sniffed. Draven passed her a napkin. She took it from him and blew her nose. "The baby. It's okay?"

I nodded. "His name is Max, and he'll be three soon." I smiled. "He's pretty darn amazing, as is my girlfriend. The thing is, Miss Johnson, Atwood is trying to take Max from us. He doesn't care about his son. What drives him is revenge, pure and simple."

She frowned. "For what?"

"Well, my girlfriend did press charges." I refrained from saying *unlike you*. I wasn't about to judge just how difficult going up against Atwood alone would have been for her. "And Atwood was found guilty and sent to prison."

A light sparked in her eyes. "He's in prison?"

"He was," I said, extinguishing the spark. "He got out on appeal, and that's when he decided to apply for custody of Max." I grazed a hand over my chin. "The courts agreed he could have visitation. This past weekend, Christa, that's my girlfriend, and I were ordered to leave Max with him. For two nights." I let that news sink in, hoping that by keeping the focus on Max, she'd relent. "I'm sure you can imagine how difficult that was for us."

She covered her mouth with her hand, her eyes filling up once more. "I can," she said, the sound muffled. "Oh God, how awful."

"So now you must be able to understand why I need your help. If you press charges, we have a shot at putting him behind bars, and this time, keeping him there."

There was a pause, the silence lingering, infusing me with hope. And then she dashed my hopes with a brief shake of her head.

"I'm so sorry, Mr. Somers." She spoke softly, barely above a whisper. "Truly, I am, but he'll say I'm crazy. I can't lose my kid."

"You won't," I insisted, even though Christa and I were in a similar position with Max, and I hadn't been able to do a damn thing to stop that. "I have the means to help you, to protect you and your daughter." I sounded desperate even to my own ears. "Please, trust me. Help me to put him away for a long time. Whatever you need. Money, a job, a safe place to stay, round-the-clock security. I can provide all of that and more."

She hesitated. I counted the silent seconds that scraped by. One, two, three, four.

And then came another curt shake of her head. "He'll either make sure I lose my little girl, or he'll kill me. And then who'll take care of Tilly? Either way, my baby loses, and I can't have that. She will always come first. I am so sorry, but I can't risk it." She scrambled to her feet. "I've got to go." She ran for the exit and disappeared.

"Fuck!" I slammed my fist into the table, causing a group of people nearby to glance briefly over their shoulders. "Goddammit."

"I did warn you," Draven said. "She's scared shitless."

"Keep looking," I barked. "If there's another Kathy Johnson out there, I want her found."

15

CHRISTA

Can you come up to my office?

I grinned. Dayton was back safe and sound. I got up from my desk and tapped on Greg's door, then poked my head inside. "Been summoned. Won't be long."

Greg smiled. "When the boss calls…"

I waggled my finger at his teasing. "I've uploaded the presentation for Friday to the shared site for your review."

"Great. I'll take a look today."

I rode the elevator up to Dayton's floor. Flashing my badge at the access-controlled glass door, I padded down the thickly carpeted hallway, smiling as I approached Angie's desk. She was on the phone but indicated for me to go straight in. I tapped the door, then entered.

Dayton's head came up, and then he rose from his chair and strolled across to greet me.

"Hey, angel." He slipped his arms around my waist and kissed me on the lips. "Missed you."

"Missed you, too."

He led me over to the conference table and pulled out a chair for me to sit. "We need to talk."

"What about?"

He took a deep breath. "I need your help."

I frowned. "With what?"

"For a few weeks now, I've had Draven poking around in Atwood's life, seeing if he can dig up anything in his background that he wouldn't want us knowing about."

I nodded. I wasn't surprised. Francesca had suggested getting a private investigator, but when Dayton hadn't mentioned it, I thought he'd decided to let the legal system play out instead.

"Why didn't you tell me?"

"Because I didn't want to worry you or get your hopes up if it all came to nothing. Call it intuition, instinct, whatever, but a guy like that, who would mandate such a vicious attack on you, had to have something in his past, something he'd rather remained buried. If shit was there, I wanted it found." He clasped my hand. "And we have."

My lips parted. "What?"

Dayton swept a hand over his face, then rubbed his lips. "Draven has discovered a woman called Kathy Johnson. That name mean anything to you?"

I shook my head. "Never heard of her."

"Well, Atwood knows her. Eleven years ago, she worked at a private members club. His father was a member, as was Atwood. He took a liking to Miss Johnson, but she wasn't interested. He followed her one night and…" Dayton bit his lip.

"Go on," I said, even though my skin prickled and a terrible unease crept over every single vertebra in my spine, one by one. I found myself sitting straighter, leaning in, wanting, but at the same time dreading for him to continue.

"He attacked her."

I narrowed my eyes. "What do you mean, attacked?"

"He raped her in every way a man can rape a woman. Then he beat her and left her lying in her own blood. A stranger found her the next morning. Got her to the hospital."

I gasped, my hand flying to my mouth. "Oh God." I closed my eyes and tried to control my escalating breathing. That poor woman. Poor, poor woman. "Is she… okay?"

A muscle in his jaw ticked. "I really don't think she is, no. I mean she walks, she breathes, but she's living a half-life, barely able to function, terrified of her own shadow. She's got a kid, a daughter—"

"His?" I interrupted, horrified.

"No. No, her daughter is only seven. What I mean is she carried on with her life, but when I met her yesterday—"

"You met her?"

He nodded, patiently accepting my multiple interjections. "Yes. And that's what I need your help with. See, at the time, she made a complaint to the police, but the Atwoods got to her, threatened her, scared her half to death, so she recanted her statement."

"And the problem went away," I finished.

"Yes."

I grimaced. "I hate that family."

He reached over to take my hand and gave it a squeeze. "You and me both, angel."

"How can I help?"

"I asked her to go to the police again, but she won't. I tried everything I could to persuade her, but she refused. She's terrified, Christa. I want you to come back to Seattle with me and talk to her. I told her what he did to you in the hope it would encourage her to cooperate. It didn't, but I think if she were to meet you, it might make a difference."

A knot formed in my stomach for what this woman must have endured, and I hated the thought of forcing her to relive it, but Dayton was right. If we could convince her to go to the police, then the case might, just might, be reopened. If Sutton was found to be culpable, that would end his contact with Max once and for all.

I looked directly into Dayton's eyes. "She'll need our help."

He nodded. "I already told her this. Whatever she needs. A safe haven, money, schooling for the kid. Anything."

I nodded. "When do we leave?"

He blew out a breath, as though he'd been worried I'd say no. "Thursday morning. I'd like to go now, but tomorrow is—"

"Sutton's day to have Max," I said, a spark of hope lighting within me that his days with my son could be numbered if, *if* I could persuade Kathy to talk.

"Yes. I want Max to come with us. If you're in agreement, I was going to ask Mrs. Flannigan if she wouldn't mind tagging along, so when we go to meet Kathy, Max can stay with her at the hotel."

"That's a good idea."

"I'll arrange it."

I stood, then nestled onto his lap. I wrapped my arms around his neck. "Thank you."

He kissed my forehead. "Thank me when that fucker is back behind bars, where he belongs."

———

The taxi pulled up outside the restaurant where Kathy Johnson was working a late shift. Draven had advised us not to call ahead in case it spooked her. Better to blindside her and hope that when faced with me, she'd at least agree to talk.

We walked inside the dimly lit restaurant. Wooden booths lined the walls, and in the middle were matching tables that seated four or six. Over each table was a low-hanging glass shade that emitted a buttery-yellow light.

"Table for two, is it?" the hostess asked, already reaching for a couple of menus.

"Actually, we're here to visit someone," I said. "Kathy Johnson."

"Oh." The girl shot me a look of disappointment, then slotted the menus back into their holder. "She's on her break. If you want to take a seat over there, I'll go see if I can find her."

I sat on the long wooden bench, but Dayton remained standing, hands stuffed in his pockets, emitting a slightly uncomfortable air. I sniggered. He met my gaze.

"What?"

"You," I said, pointing my chin at him. "If this was the Waldorf Astoria, you'd be in your element. But here... fish out of water."

He arched a brow. "Are you teasing me, Ms. Adams?"

"Maybe," I drawled.

He chuckled, then sat beside me, his long legs splayed out in front of him, his ankles crossed. "Better?"

"Not really. Now you just look uncomfortable seated." I bit my lip. "Sorry, I don't mean to make jokes. I'm just nervous about meeting her, that's all."

He smiled. "The stakes are high. I get it. Nothing wrong with alleviating a hideous situation with a bit of humor." Something caught his eye, and he nudged me with his elbow. "There she is."

I tracked his gaze to a petite redhead dressed in a blue uniform and scuffed black flats. Dear God, she wouldn't have stood a chance against Sutton. She must be almost a foot shorter, and slight. One hundred and ten pounds at most. My heart clenched, then stuttered, empathy for her suffering rushing through me. I rose to my feet as she turned her attention our way. She spotted Dayton first, and her jaw clenched. She whispered something to the girl who'd gone to fetch her, then shook her head.

I touched Dayton's arm. "Wait here." I strode over, conscious that if I didn't act quickly, she might run. "Kathy," I said. "Please, I just need a few minutes of your time."

Kathy glanced between me and Dayton, and then she turned to her friend. "It's okay, Marsha. I got this."

"I'm right over there, sweetie."

Marsha returned to her position behind the podium, leaving me alone with Kathy. She nibbled her lip and wrung her hands. "I already told your boyfriend, I can't help you."

"Yes, he said. And I respect that, truly, I do. All I'm asking for is five minutes. Just to talk. I'm so, so sorry for what Sutton did to you, for how, even years later, you're still suffering. I've been there. I'm still there. You and me? We know how evil and destructive that man is. Please, just give me five minutes."

Kathy's gaze flickered between me and the floor. She rubbed the middle of her forehead, then shook her head as if she was about to refuse.

"If we stand together, we have a chance of beating him. Please, at least hear me... us out." I gestured to Dayton who'd, sensibly, stayed back.

She paused, then gave a brief nod. "I don't get off until ten. We can talk then."

I glanced at my watch. Eight-thirty. "We can wait."

"Okay." She spun on her heel and disappeared into what I presumed was the kitchen. I returned to where Dayton was still sprawled on the bench in an attempt to appear relaxed. I stopped at the podium.

"It seems we'll be needing that table after all," I said to Marsha.

Dayton sprang to his feet. "What?"

I smiled weakly. He'd hate eating here. Tex-mex fare definitely wasn't his thing. I opened the menu that Marsha passed to me. "Oh look, a bucket of wings. My favorite."

Dayton's eyes widened. I slipped my arm through his. "We'll take that booth in the corner." I followed Marsha to the table, tugging a reluctant Dayton behind me.

Marsha set down two sets of silverware wrapped in a thin paper napkin. "Your server will be over shortly to take your drinks order."

"Thanks," I said, reaching for the list of drinks. "Shall we have a bottle of wine?"

"Not fucking likely," Dayton said, his lip curled in distaste as he scanned the menu. "They only sell a house white." He shuddered. "Urgh."

I couldn't help but smile. "You are such a snob," I whispered.

I ordered a margarita, and Dayton reluctantly chose a Manhattan. The server returned after a few minutes, set down our cocktails, then took our food order.

"Remind me again why we're eating here when there's a perfectly good restaurant five minutes' walk away?" Dayton asked once the server had left.

"Because Kathy doesn't get off until ten."

"And? We could still have eaten there and then returned here in time to meet with her."

"And risk her slipping out the door? No, it's better we're here, in plain sight. Plus, if she sees that we're just normal people…" I paused and raked my gaze over him. "Correction. If she sees that *I'm* normal, she might relax a little, and I'll have a better chance of reassuring her."

He gave me an affronted glare. "I'm normal. I just have good taste."

I smiled and patted his arm. "Yes, you do."

He captured my wrist and brought my hand to his mouth. He pressed a soft kiss to my knuckles. "I hope you can get her to agree to press charges."

"Me, too. But listen, I think I should talk to her alone."

"Why?"

I sipped my drink, pondering whether I should share the thoughts I'd had at our first meeting. "Did I ever tell you that the first time I met you, my instinct was to run?"

His eyes opened wide. "No."

I nodded. "When Jake brought me to your office, my first thought was that you reminded me of Sutton. Powerful, domineering, rich. The kind of person I wanted to have nothing to do with. I think Kathy sees the same things in you that I did."

His jaw tightened. "I am *nothing* like that scum."

"No, you're not. But the reason I know that is because I know you. Kathy doesn't. All she sees is another moneyed, authoritarian guy who's trying to force her into reliving what, for her, was the worst day of her life. I understand her fear because it was my fear. I lived through what they put her through. The threats, the intimidation, the constant looking over your shoulder, waiting for the next metaphorical—or very real—blow to be struck. Terrified that you're not strong enough to hold on. Reliving the horror over and over and over."

He let out a long breath of air. "I never thought of it like that." He circled his middle finger around the rim of his glass, lost in thought. "Do you think other people see me like that?"

"No. I think Kathy and I have a skewed view of men in power, but that's because of our experiences. There are countless other broke guys out there who are equally evil. It's not the money that makes the man, Dayton. Sutton would have been the same malevolent psychopath if he had to eat from garbage cans to stay alive. The only difference is that his money enabled him to get away with it."

My reassurances seemed to calm him, and we spent the rest of the waiting time talking about work, Max, anything but Sutton Atwood. At five after ten, Kathy appeared over by the bar. She'd changed into ripped jeans, a T-shirt, and a pair of red chucks that had definitely seen better days. I'd seen her watching us from time to time as she worked, and when she headed over, she appeared slightly less spooked.

Dayton rose to his feet. "I'll wait at the bar. Leave you ladies to talk."

"I can't stay long," Kathy said. "I gotta get back for my Tilly." She waited until he'd left, then slid into the seat he'd vacated.

"Thank you for agreeing to talk to me," I said. "Would you like a drink?"

She shook her head and nibbled on a thumbnail that was already bitten right down to the soft skin at the tip. She had an air of exhaustion surrounding her, a beaten-down look, and my heart squeezed painfully.

"Your boyfriend said you was attacked, too."

I nodded. "I was, although my experience was different to yours."

"Yeah, you wasn't raped, he said."

"No. Beaten, but not raped."

I kept my answers purposely short because I wanted her to ask the questions, to allow her to control the pace. I wasn't about to push her. She was skittish enough as it was, her gaze darting around, not quite meeting my eyes. I wondered if she'd been like this before Sutton had viciously assaulted her, or whether her current demeanor was a result of the attack.

"Are you still scared?" she asked.

It was an interesting question, one that gave me insight into her psyche. I paused, taking a sip of my drink as a distraction technique while I thought of the right thing to say. Our circumstances were completely different. I'd been lucky, I'd found Dayton. This poor woman was all alone, struggling to bring up a child on minimum wage and probably suffering from a form of PTSD, especially if she hadn't received the right kind of help at the time of the assault.

"Sometimes I still wake up in a sweat, my heart drumming against my ribcage, my breathing out of control, but it's rarer these days." When that happened, I'd curl into Dayton's side, and he'd soothe me, his palm rubbing comforting circles on my back until my heartrate returned to normal and the terrible sense of fear receded.

"Because you have him." She cocked her head toward Dayton who'd settled himself at the bar, his back to us.

I nodded. "I was lucky."

"He's not like *him* then?"

I noticed she never used Sutton's name. I wondered sometimes why I found it so easy to. Maybe because I'd once been in a relationship with him. "No. He's nothing like Sutton."

She leaned forward, a spark of interest in her eyes. "Your boyfriend said you was beaten and mutilated, but not by *him*. By someone else."

"Yes. He paid someone to beat me and cut me." I laughed bitterly.

"Wonder why he didn't do it himself?" Kathy mused, although I wasn't sure whether the question was for me or for herself. Maybe she was trying to figure out why she'd been different.

"I don't know. I gave up trying to figure out Sutton Atwood long ago."

"He's a madman," she said matter-of-factly.

"Yes. He is. And now he's trying to take my son."

"His kid."

I shook my head violently. "No. Max is *mine*. I never wanted him to have anything to do with his father. Ten years he got. Ten years in prison for what he did to me. I thought we were safe. I thought I could move on." My voice hitched, and I cleared my throat. "Sorry. I just don't know what to do. That's why I need your help."

Kathy got up and, for a brief moment, I thought I'd scared her away. Instead, she came around to my side of the table and sat next to me. She put her arm around my shoulder and hugged me, resting her head on top of mine. We fell into silence, two women with the most heinous of things in common.

"I want to help you—honest to God I do—but I know what he's capable of. I can't go through that again. I can't risk him hurting Tilly, or me. I gotta be there for my daughter. I'm all she's got." She squeezed me tighter. "I'm real sorry you've come all this way for nothin'."

The worst part about hearing Kathy refuse my request was that I understood. If I'd been in her position, I would have probably felt the same. I could spew out all the platitudes, tell her we'd protect her, that she'd be safe, blah blah blah, but that's all they'd be. Words. I was proof that when Sutton Atwood had you in his sights, he didn't let go. She'd escaped, and she wanted it to stay that way. If she came back onto his radar, who knew what he'd do? I could keep trying to persuade her, but one look at the set of her jaw, and the determination sound in her tone, I knew I'd be wasting my time.

"It wasn't for nothing," I said, touching my head to hers briefly. "I got to meet you, and for that, I'm glad."

I took a card out of my pocket, one I'd written my number on earlier. I passed it to her. "If you need anything at all. Ever. Call me. No strings."

She took it from me, rose from the bench, and slipped it in her back pocket.

"You're a good person. I hope you find a way to stop him."

I tracked her as she left the restaurant, then I cut my eyes to Dayton. I gave a small shake of my head.

No joy.

16

DAYTON

I KISSED the top of Christa's head. "We're here."

She yawned and stretched, then turned sleepy eyes toward me. "Did I sleep the whole way?"

I nodded. "Pretty much."

"Some company I am."

"That's okay. Max, Mrs. Flannigan, and I entertained ourselves, didn't we, buddy?"

"Yep," Max said, emphasizing the 'P'.

"I still can't believe I got to fly in this amazing plane," Mrs. Flannigan said excitedly. "Wait until I tell my husband, although he won't believe me."

I smiled, even though I wasn't feeling it on the inside. I couldn't shake my disappointment that Kathy had refused to go to the police. I'd been sure that confronted with Christa, and knowing what he'd done to her, understanding that Kathy wasn't his only victim, she'd have capitulated. I could empathize with her fear, but still...

"We'll find another way," Christa murmured.

I squeezed her hand as we taxied to a stop. "I know."

Except I didn't know. Whatever I did, however many strings

I pulled or people I paid, victory edged out of my grasp. Max wasn't an object we were fighting over, but I had no doubt we were in the middle of a war, and one I could not, *would not* lose.

Paul was waiting outside the car at the bottom of the airplane steps. Mrs. Flannigan insisted on sitting up front, said she felt more comfortable there. I shrugged. Made no difference to me. I fastened Max into his car seat and got in the back with Christa.

"I'll have Paul drive you home first, Mrs. Flannigan," I said as he pulled away.

"Actually," Christa said. "Would you mind looking after Max today?"

I gave Christa a quizzical frown.

"Not at all," Mrs. Flannigan said. "We can take a walk in the park. It's too lovely to be cooped up inside."

"Park!" Max shouted. "Ponies."

He loved stroking the horses lined up around Central Park. Maybe when he was older, I'd get him a pony of his own. There were stables not far from my home in the Catskills where we could keep the thing.

"I need to work," she explained, holding her hand in the air when I opened my mouth to tell her no, she fucking didn't. "I'm going in for my third surgery on Monday."

The hideous word Atwood had Christa's attacker score into her stomach had gone, but she still had a few more skin grafts to go in order to diminish the scarring.

"I'm well aware of that. I don't see the relevance."

"I'm busy, Dayton. Greg is pitching to a new client next week, and I'm pulling the presentation together."

"I'll have someone else assigned."

She narrowed her eyes and fixed her jaw in the manner I'd come to recognize as Christa getting ready to put her foot down. "No, you won't. This is *my* account and *my* hard work that's got us to this point. I'm not bailing at the last minute. It's bad enough I won't be there for the actual meeting." She nibbled her lip. "In fact, I'd been considering putting off the surgery to allow me to go."

"Not a chance," I said, my voice rising in volume.

Mrs. Flannigan's head twitched, indicating interest in our conversation, so I pressed the button on the center console, and the privacy screen activated. "Your health, those surgeries, come before any client. There will be other clients, other pitches, other presentations. You will be having the surgery on Monday, and you *will* be taking the next two weeks off."

She glared at me. "You can pull that arrogant bullshit with other people all you like, but not with me. If I choose to put off *my* surgery, then that's *my* choice."

I widened my eyes at her vehement outburst. It wasn't like Christa to be so combative, and it demonstrated the strain she was under because of this fucking Atwood debacle and what she saw as her failure to persuade Kathy to come forward.

I caught her hand and rubbed my thumb over her knuckles. "Bad choice of words. Of course it's your decision whether you go in for surgery or not, but what I meant to say is work should not come before your health."

"Says the workaholic," she grumbled, adding, " anyway, I only said considering."

"So, you'll have the surgery?"

She sighed heavily. "Yes. But I'm still working this afternoon. And I can work from home after the surgery."

"No," I insisted. "You need to recuperate. You're taking two full weeks off." I spotted the look on her face. "I'm not kidding, Christa."

She huffed, exasperated. "Sitting at a desk, tapping on a computer isn't exactly physically taxing."

"But it is mentally exhausting. The answer is still no."

She turned to stare out of the window, muttering under her breath, "You'll be at the office anyway, so I can do what I want."

I ground my teeth. God, she could be frustrating as hell at

times. I removed my phone and pulled up my calendar. One or two meetings might give me a bit of a headache to rearrange, but the rest...

I called Angie. "I'll be working at home for the next two weeks, Angie." Christa's head whipped round, her eyes wide. "Have the location of all my meetings changed to the penthouse, with the exception of the one with Senator Austin. That location remains as is."

"Don't be so ridiculous," Christa hissed through her teeth.

I ignored her. "Tell Frank he's got the chair. Put in a meeting at six each evening for us to catch up."

"Yes, Mr. Somers."

I cut the call.

Christa folded her arms and shifted her body so she was turned away from me. "You are so exasperating at times."

"I get it from you," I hit back.

The atmosphere in the car chilled, and Christa ignored me for the rest of the journey home. The second we walked into the penthouse, she went straight to work, setting up her laptop at the dining table, her back pointedly to me. I opened my mouth to make an attempt at reconciliation, but at the last moment, I changed my mind. Instead, I left her to it and went to my study to update Draven.

"No luck," I said when he answered.

A resigned sigh filtered down the line. "I'm not surprised. Poor bitch is scared shitless."

"Yep, but this makes it even more important that we keep looking. If Atwood had a penchant for attacking girls in his youth, even if he progressed to getting others to do his dirty work later in life, there are more like Kathy out there. I know it. All we have to do is find them."

"I'm on it," Draven said. "I won't stop until we nail the fucker."

My eyes sprang open, and it took me a few seconds to realize that my phone was ringing. I groaned and rolled onto my side. Three-fifteen in the goddamn morning. I felt around in the darkness, finally closing my hand around my cell.

"What?" I snapped as Christa stirred beside me.

"Dayton." Nina's urgent voice came down the phone. "It's Dad. He's had a heart attack."

I sat up and flicked the bedside lamp on. "So?" I said, waiting to feel something, but inside was only emptiness. I'd given up caring about my father a long time ago, and the fact he was laid up in the hospital, maybe about to die, didn't change a thing. I had much more important things on my mind than the man who'd beaten the living crap out of me and my sister for years, then tossed me out onto the street with nothing and no means to look after myself. He could rot for all I gave a shit.

"Dayton," Nina pleaded. "I need to go see him before it's too late. I need closure."

Christa touched my arm, concern darkening her features, our earlier fight forgotten. "What's going on?"

"My so-called father has had a heart attack."

Christa sat up. "Oh no."

"I'm coming home," Nina said. "I'll be there in three hours." When I didn't respond, she yelled, "Dayton! This might be the last chance we have to understand why he behaved the way he did."

"I don't care for his platitudes or his excuses, because there is nothing that man could say that would justify what he did."

"Please, Dayton," Nina said. "Don't make me do this alone. I need you. If I'm going to pluck up the courage to face him, I need you by my side."

I clenched my jaw. Nina knew she was one of the few people

I found it hard to say no to, and she'd played her trump card to perfection.

"Fine," I said. "I'll pick you up from the airport and then I'll take you to the hospital."

"Thank you," she said. "I love you."

She ended our call before I could tell her I loved her, too. I dropped the phone in my lap and rubbed my hands over my face. "Fucking wonderful."

"Is he going to die?" Christa asked.

"I hope so," I said, causing her to frown. "Slowly and painfully."

"You don't mean that."

I laughed bitterly. "That's just it. I do mean it. I hate him, Christa. Like *hate* him. Nina has always had an urge to know why he treated us so badly, why he chose my sixteenth birthday to throw me out, but I never have. Do you want to know why?" She nodded. "Because there *is* no reason. He's just a vicious bully who got off on beating his kids. Maybe it was some sort of power trip, but there is nothing he could say to me now that would make me forgive him. Nothing." I threw back the covers and climbed out of bed. "Some people are just born bad, Christa. You had the misfortune to hook up with one, and I had the misfortune to be bred by one. But believing people like that can be redeemed... I don't buy it. If my father thinks that confessing his sins will allow him to die in peace, you can fucking bet I will take great pleasure in denying him that." I bent over and kissed her. "Go back to sleep. I'll call you from the hospital."

"Do you want me to come with you?"

I shook my head. "Hanging around a hospital is no place for Max. Besides, I won't be there long."

She shot me a concerned look but did as I'd asked, snuggling back under the covers. I flicked off the light, casting the room back into darkness.

When the time came for me to fetch Nina, I accessed the

garage via my private elevator and scanned the rows of cars. My eyes alighted on my latest toy—a sleek black sports car imported from Germany. I grabbed the keys from the cabinet and climbed inside. The smell of new leather tickled my nostrils, and the dark, compact interior sent a shiver of excitement through me. A fast ride out to the airfield in a car that needed a firm hand was just the thing to take my mind off my fucking father. I turned the key in the ignition, and the engine roared to life, rumbling under the hood, vibrating my seat.

I pushed the shift into first then eased her up the ramp that led outside. Manhattan hadn't quite woken up, so the streets weren't rammed with cars, allowing me to open the throttle. As I drove out to the private airfield to pick up Nina, the tension that had been riding me these last few weeks ebbed away. I needed this, the freedom of the open road, being in control of a demanding car, the smell of burning rubber as I pushed her to her limits.

By the time I parked alongside the plane, I felt calmer, more centered, better equipped to deal with what was to come. Seconds after I arrived, Nina came running down the aluminum steps. She greeted me by throwing herself into my arms.

"Thank you for agreeing to come with me. I can't do this alone."

I kissed her forehead. "You know I'll do anything for you." I opened the passenger door, then strode around the front of the car to get in the driver's side. "Nina, listen. I don't want you to get your hopes up that he'll be contrite or able to explain away his actions. He won't, even if he's well enough to talk, because there are no excuses for what he did to us. You may want closure, but you're not going to get it."

She closed her hand over mine where it was rested on the steering wheel. "I thought about this a lot on the flight over. And you're right. I don't think there is a reason. But I decided that closure for me is simply being able to look my father in the eye and show him he didn't win. Stand before him so he can see I'm happy, healthy, and living a full life, despite the trauma of my childhood. *That's* my closure."

I nodded, understanding. "Mine is watching that fucker take his last breath, then putting him in the ground where his body can slowly rot. Where I can imagine his flesh being eaten by maggots and smile to myself."

She winced. "You paint quite the picture, brother."

I started the engine. "Sorry." I wasn't sorry, though, not for any of it. I wanted that man to die screaming in agony and begging for my forgiveness. It wouldn't happen, but it made me happy to imagine.

We drove to the hospital in silence. I let Nina out at the entrance, then went to find a parking spot. By the time I joined her in reception, she'd found out where he was. We rode the elevator up to the fourth floor, to the ICU. Once we explained to the nurse on duty who we were, she showed us to his room.

I placed the palm of my hand on the small of Nina's back and eased her inside. It had been years since I'd seen my father, and the intervening time had not been kind. He'd lost at least thirty pounds, his skin was thinning, his hair almost gone. Broken capillaries across his nose and cheeks made a crisscross pattern, and they had me wondering if he'd turned to excessive drinking in the last few years.

He was hooked up to several machines, some emitting a low bleeping sound, others silent. He looked small, insignificant, his power eroded by age. I waited to feel something, anything, even pleasure, but inside was only emptiness. I guess I'd avenged us years ago, and now there was nothing left to feel.

Nina edged forward, peering over him. "God, Dayton, he... he doesn't even look like I remembered. He looks so... different. Nothing like the towering man who'd scared me so." She pulled up a chair and lowered herself onto it.

I remained standing. "Is he going to die?" I asked the nurse who was sitting quietly in the corner, resting a clipboard with a pen dangling from a piece of string on her lap.

She offered me a sympathetic smile. "We're doing all we can."

"That doesn't answer my question."

Her eyes widened at the sharpness of my tone. Nina shot me an irritated glare, then slowly shook her head. She was used to me.

"He's a very sick man," the nurse said, her lips pursing in annoyance. "He suffered a massive heart attack, and he's old and frail."

"So, that's a yes then," I drawled. "He is going to die."

She stared at me as though I was an unfeeling monster. I wanted to point at my father and yell, "Well, there's your fucking cause."

"We're not hopeful he'll recover, no."

Good. I rested my hands on Nina's shoulders and stared at my childhood torturer, willing him to Just. Fucking. Die. I didn't need this shit diverting my focus away from Atwood.

"Dad," Nina said. "Can you hear me? I'm here, and Dayton is, too."

"Under duress," I muttered.

Nina didn't respond to my childish murmurings. "Come on, Dad. Open your eyes."

A rattle echoed through his chest and—fuck me—his lids flickered, then opened. That merciless gaze locked on to me, and for a few seconds, the heartless bastard made a comeback. My hatred for him was only mirrored by his for me. There was no reason for his past behavior. He was a sadist, that was all, a man who took pleasure in causing others pain.

He was another fucking Atwood.

"That's it, Dad," Nina whispered, misreading the animosity in his eyes for determination, a desire to live. "It's me, Nina."

The nurse rose from her chair and pressed her fingers to his wrist.

His eyes flickered to Nina's but didn't linger. No, it was me he wanted to focus on. Me, who he truly abhorred. He'd treated Nina badly because he knew how much it hurt me to see my sister frightened, cowering in the corner. I'd never tell her that, though. I refused to break her that way.

I met his gaze head-on, my message clear. He beckoned me forward. I stepped around Nina and leaned over him.

"You're going to die tonight," I whispered in his ear. "And I'm going to enjoy watching you suffer."

He coughed, spittle dribbling down his chin. I left it there. This man didn't deserve any sympathy, any care or attention.

"Dayton." His voice sounded as if he was talking through a pit of gravel, raw and husky and barely audible. "I might be about to die, but I don't care because while my suffering will be over, yours will persist. I'll continue to live on through your hatred for me."

I straightened to find him staring at me, eyes bulging, not through regret or distress, but through pure loathing.

I curled my lips into a sneer and put my mouth right by his ear once more. "Rot in Hell."

He began to cough violently. Machines went off, the beeping sounds piercing my ears. And then Nina and I were shoved out of the way as medical personnel piled into the room.

I stood at the back watching them work on him, but I knew he wouldn't make it. And I refused to feel a moment of sorrow.

Good. Fucking. Riddance.

17

CHRISTA

I SLIPPED my arm through Dayton's as we stood at the graveside, watching his father's coffin being lowered into the ground. There was only the three of us in attendance: me, Dayton, and Nina. Some of Dayton's father's old business contacts had offered to come along, but Dayton had stipulated immediate family only.

He'd also insisted on a burial, although I'd always thought them macabre. The idea of being eaten by bugs and stuff, even if I was dead... Urgh...

Dayton hadn't shed a single tear or shown any grief at his father's passing. Then again, after what his dad did to him when he was just a child, I wasn't surprised he couldn't find forgiveness in his heart but, all the same, I worried about the level of stress he was under. However much he hated his father, he had still lost a parent, not to mention the looming threat of Sutton and our inability to find a way to beat him. I touched his elbow, and he glanced down at me, the skin around his mouth tight, crinkles around his eyes. He looked tired and withdrawn, and my heart ached for him.

There would be no reception, no period of mourning, following today's service. From Dayton's perspective, he'd done his duty by arranging the funeral. I'd half expected him to refuse to attend, but when I'd asked him, he'd muttered something about being there for Nina and making sure his father was truly gone.

The minister said a few words, but as I glanced up at Dayton's clenched jaw and fixed expression, I wasn't sure if he was even listening. After it was over, we headed back to the car. I winced as I climbed inside. My wound was still a little raw after surgery last week.

"You shouldn't have come," Dayton said when he spotted my discomfort. "You should be at home, resting."

"It's fine." I gestured dismissively. He'd been smothering me all week, and while I appreciated how attentive he was, sometimes I just wanted him to give me some space. "Besides, I wanted to be here to support you." I clipped my seat belt in place, holding it away from my stomach, and rested my head back against the seat. I did feel exhausted, not that I was about to tell Dayton that. He'd become insufferable if he knew how much I was struggling.

Nina had remained tight-lipped about her feelings, and as she sat across from me in the back of Dayton's limousine, my concern for her grew. The death of her father had definitely hit her much harder than it had Dayton. She appeared drained, the tips of her fingers pinching at her throat as she stared out the window, and she'd lost some weight since his passing last week.

I leaned forward and squeezed her knee. "How you holding up?"

She gave me a faint smile. "Glad that part's over."

Ever since I'd known her, Nina had always had such a happy disposition, so to see her quiet and withdrawn, it worried me. "I'm here if you want to talk."

"Why would she want to talk?" Dayton cut in. "He's gone, and that's a good thing."

Nina winced. I shot a glare in Dayton's direction. He might

be relieved his father had passed away, but Nina's feelings were entirely different. I shifted in my seat. Pain shot through my abdomen and I repressed a hiss. "Because she's not you," I said. "And women process things completely differently than men. So pipe down and keep your thoughts about what Nina may or may not want to yourself."

The first smile I'd seen in a week broke on Nina's face, her expression the complete opposite of Dayton's. "I love you, Christa," she said. "You're exactly what my can-sometimes-be-a-complete-ass brother needs."

"Well, someone has to keep him in check." I shook my head. "Honestly, Dayton, you don't have to vocalize every thought in your head."

A spluttering laugh erupted from Nina, this time probably because of the incensed expression on Dayton's face.

"Jesus," he muttered. "I'll shut up then, yeah?"

"That'd be best," I said condescendingly. I even added a shoulder pat.

"You're priceless," Nina said, wiping a stray tear away, although I was certain this one was brought on by laughter.

I held out my pinkie. "Us girls gotta stick together."

Nina giggled and twisted her pinkie around mine. The mood inside the car lifted at our mutual goading of Dayton, which had been my intention.

"When are you going back to Chicago?" Dayton asked, clearly fed up with us.

Nina twirled a lock of hair around her finger, teasing him. "I'd planned to head back tomorrow, but I may stick around a bit longer." She winked at me. "That's okay, isn't it?"

"I suppose so," he grumbled, then proceeded to stare out the window.

"I think Nina should stay for the rest of the week," I said, turning to Dayton. "That way, you could go into the office, rather than stay home keeping an eye on me."

Dayton locked gazes with me, his eyes narrowing. "Anyone would think you wanted to get rid of me."

"Of course I don't," I said, knowing he'd be hurt if I told him I craved some space. "But you've got to admit, it's been difficult for you to work from home this week. You need to be at the sharp end, where you can keep an eye on things."

Dayton nodded, deep in thought. "Would you be okay staying the week?" he asked Nina.

"Absolutely. I can work from your penthouse more easily than you can. I'm remote whether I'm at your place or the Manhattan office. And I'll get to spend time with Max, too."

"Okay." He felt for my hand, squeezing it. "As long as you're in agreement with that."

"Works for me," I said, trying not to smile too broadly. With Dayton out of the way, I could work longer hours than he'd allowed this week. I was in the middle of developing some new software code, and I needed peace and quiet—rather than him breathing down my neck to finish it. When I returned to the office next week, I wanted it ready to demo to Greg.

He lifted my hand to his mouth and kissed my knuckles. "Then it works for me."

———

I slowly lowered myself down onto the bed, my back to Dayton so he couldn't see me wincing. Today had taken more out of me than I cared to admit, but I remembered from the last two rounds of surgery that the first week was the worst. From here on, I should start to feel a whole lot better.

I tucked the covers around my legs and picked up a book I'd been reading about software engineering. Dayton had his iPad resting on bent legs, tapping away, probably answering emails. He worked too damned hard, but with the time out he'd taken to help me deal with Sutton, the trips back and forth to Seattle, as well as this sorry business with his father, I knew he felt out of the loop. That was another reason I wanted him to go back to the office this week.

"I think you should talk to Nina."

He paused, mid-type, and twisted his head to look at me. "About what?"

I kept my eyes on my book, even though I wasn't really paying attention. "About your father."

He expelled a long, drawn-out sigh, and swept a hand over his face. "What's the point? He's dead."

I let the book fall onto my lap. "That's exactly the point."

His brows drew low into a deep frown. "I'm not following."

"I could be wrong, which is why I think you should talk to her, but I'm worried she regrets that she didn't try to reconcile with your father, and now it's too late."

His eyes opened wide, and he sat up straighter. His iPad fell onto the bed with a *thunk*.

"When I picked Nina up at the airport, she told me that closure for her was to look him in the eye and show him he hadn't won. That she was happy despite his best efforts to the contrary, which is exactly what she did when we were at the hospital. She hates my father as much as I do."

"Does she? Have you asked her?"

"I don't need to ask her."

"Helpful," I said, unable to keep sarcasm from bleeding into my tone.

He gave the smallest shake of his head. "I don't mean to be dismissive, but what would it achieve? Nothing. All it'll do is drag up memories that are best left buried with that fucker."

I nibbled on my lip. I had a theory, but he wasn't going to like it. "I think Nina stayed away from your father because of you."

His forehead creased, and his eyebrows shot up. "Me?"

I nodded. "She is well aware how much you hate him, and

she put your feelings first. I'm not saying she doesn't hate him, too, for what he did to you both, but I also think Nina is more empathetic than you are. I think she desperately wanted to try and understand *why* he treated you both so badly, what his reasons were for throwing you out on the street with little more than the clothes on your back, and now she'll never know."

His jaw tightened, and I could hear the sound of bone and enamel grinding together. "My father was a bastard. Pure and simple. I won't sit here and pretend to mourn for a man I abhorred. And as for his reasons…" He snorted. "There are *no* *excuses* for what he did. I don't see what good going over old ground would do either me or Nina."

"Talking about it might help you both move on."

"I have fucking moved on!"

He raked a hand through his hair while I sat in silence. He'd done no such thing, but he had to come to that realization on his own.

Seconds turned into minutes, but I refused to look away, and eventually, Dayton met my gaze. His eyes were bleak, his shoulders curved. "I can't forgive him, Christa. I *won't*."

"I know," I said softly. "And I'm not asking you to."

Dayton's ability to hold a grudge, to keep going until he served his own brand of justice, was the very thing I was relying on to help me beat Sutton. But at the same time, I wanted him to recognize that holding on to hatred for his father, especially now that he'd passed, would destroy him in the end. He'd already won. He'd beaten the man who'd abused him for all those years and, now his father was dead, Dayton had to let that shit go.

"But what I am saying is that you need to be there for Nina and, by helping her come to terms with her grief—and her regrets that she didn't reach out to your father before it was too late—will heal your own wounds. *Then*, and only then, will you truly leave all this behind you."

He blinked, and then nodded. "Okay, I'll talk to her. Now will you drop it, please?"

I put my book on the nightstand, then curled into Dayton's side. I gave him a goofy grin. "Consider it dropped."

I loved winning our little tiffs.

18

DAYTON

I DID AS CHRISTA ASKED—CORRECTION, insisted—and spoke to Nina. I'd always considered us to be extremely close, but when she cried in my arms and told me she wished she'd at least tried to get through to our father—confirming Christa's suspicions—I felt like an absolute fucker. My hatred for him, and her love for me, had meant she'd let the days, weeks, months, and years slide by, all the while harboring an urge to at least try.

But I didn't regret a single action. If Nina spent the rest of her life blaming me, thinking that it was my fault she didn't feel able to reach out to him, I'd take it, because it was far, far preferable to the alternative—that she'd have been exposed to his vile, blackened soul.

I hadn't told her what he'd said to me before he'd died, or the look I'd seen in his eyes as he'd taken his final breaths—that I'd witnessed the full extent of his vicious core as it exposed itself with shuddering clarity. He hadn't cared about us because he'd never had it within him to care. Charles Loxton Somers had only given a shit about one person, and that was himself. His final words to me were testament to that. He loved to see me suffer. I wouldn't give him the satisfaction of a single moment of empathy.

Christa had been right to urge me to talk to Nina, because it allowed my sister to get it all off her chest. By the time I dropped her at the private airfield on Friday afternoon, she was standing a little taller, her spine erect, color had returned to her cheeks, and her gorgeous smile was firmly back in place.

"Call me when you land," I said, leaning forward to peck her cheek.

"I will. Tell Christa I'll give her a ring over the weekend. I know she's dreading tonight."

A surge of anger tightened my jaw, and my stomach formed into knots. Atwood's second weekend with Max. Fuck, had it only been three weeks since we'd gone to Niagara and received the call I'd hoped would change everything? *Well, that had been a waste of fucking time, hadn't it?* And *still* there was nothing further from Draven. Every day that passed I lost a little more hope that we'd find a way to get Atwood out of our lives for good. Even if there were more Kathys out there, we had to find them first. Then we had to persuade them to relive the worst time in their lives and potentially come face to face with a man who'd done unspeakable things to them, all to help someone they didn't know.

The chances of pulling that off were tantamount to winning the fucking lottery.

"Yeah, we both are." I rubbed my chin. "I hate that fucker. I despise what he did to Christa, and it kills me that we have to let Max go with him, and there isn't a damned thing we can do about it."

Nina hugged me. "Love you both so much, and the little man. Give him a big kiss from his Aunty Nina."

I watched as she walked up the steps to the plane. She turned around at the top and waved, blew me a kiss, then disappeared inside.

My phone buzzed in my pocket. I answered it without looking at the screen. "Somers."

"It's Draven. Are you sitting down?"

My heart began to gallop, and a prickling sensation caused me to flex my fingers. "Go on."

"I found another Kathy."

I slammed my fist on the roof of my car. "I fucking *knew* it. When do we go talk to her?"

"We don't," Draven said.

I frowned. "Why the fuck not?"

"Because she's dead."

My mouth dropped open, and then, as the shock receded, disappointment twisted my insides. I pinched the bridge of my nose between my thumb and forefinger and took a deep breath to calm the storm swirling in my gut. "How did she die?"

"Suicide."

Fuck!

"Then what's the point of this call?" I snapped, my frustration not aimed at Draven but at the run of bad luck we were having, at the unfairness of this whole situation. At Sutton *Fucking* Atwood.

"I'm calling because her family has agreed to talk to you," Draven ground out. "Her name is—was—Sunny, and she killed herself exactly one year after Atwood assaulted her. That was nine years ago. Her parents found her hanging in her bedroom. She was nineteen."

Nausea churned in my stomach, and I clasped a hand around my middle. "So he did it again, after Kathy?"

"Seems like it, yeah. Probably waited until the heat died down before picking another victim."

"Jesus." I scraped a hand through my hair. The engines fired up on Nina's plane, making it difficult to talk. "Hang on a sec." I got in the car, turned the ignition, then drove away. "You still there?"

"Yeah." Draven's voice came through the car speakers. "I'm gonna keep searching for more victims. I doubt he suddenly developed a conscience. I'll email what I know and text you the address and phone number for Sunny's parents. They're expecting your call."

"Thanks." I pressed a button on the dash, cutting the call. A few seconds later, my phone dinged with a text from Draven, giving me the details.

"Jesus, fuck, bastard!" I whacked the steering wheel. I'd thought my father had been evil, but he was Mother fucking Theresa when compared to Atwood. Poor Sunny. Poor, poor kid. I could not imagine feeling that your life was so worthless, it was better to end it all rather than continue on.

I drove home, breaking several speed limits. I launched out of the car, jogged over to the private elevator, and punched in the code. On the way up, I scanned Draven's email. The details were scant, but I was hoping her parents could fill in the gaps.

"Christa?" I called out as soon as I entered the living room.

She appeared at the far end of the hallway, outside Max's room. "I'm here. Just getting his bag ready." Her mouth turned down at the edges, and there was a bow to her spine. "Everything okay with Nina?"

"Yeah. We talked. I'll update you later." I went to join her, picking Max up and throwing him over my shoulder. His peals of laughter lightened the weight in my heart. "Listen, when Max has gone, I need to talk to you."

She put the last of his things in his overnight bag, then zipped it up. "Everything okay?"

I nodded. "Let's deal with this first."

Atwood arrived, right on time. I ground my teeth as the elevator doors opened and he swaggered out. I glared at him, seeing him through a different lens. I'd always known he was a psychopath who derived enormous pleasure from hurting others, especially Christa, but now, I also knew he was a rapist and, in my eyes, a murderer. If he hadn't attacked Sunny, she wouldn't have taken her own life.

"Hey, Max," he said, crouching to Max's level. "Ready to go?"

As he put his filthy, rapist hands on the child I'd come to think of as my own, I almost lost it. Almost. I held it together by the skin of my teeth and by digging my fingernails into my palms until I drew blood. Normally, I'd put a brave face on, for Max's sake, but today, I just didn't have it in me.

"See you later, bud," I said, trying—and failing—to muster a smile. I spun around and went inside my penthouse, not trusting myself to remain in the company of that animal for a second longer.

Christa joined me a couple of minutes later. "What's going on?" she demanded.

"Draven's found another girl."

Christa gasped, but I carried on. "Except this one killed herself a year after Atwood raped her."

Her hand flew to her mouth. "Oh God," she said, the sound coming out all muffled. She clasped her knees and bent over. "I think I'm going to be sick."

I caught her before her legs gave out and helped her through to the living room. Placing her gently on the couch, I then fetched her a glass of water. I sat beside her as she sipped. Once she'd had enough, and her nausea had retreated, I put the glass on the coffee table and clasped her hand.

"The parents are willing to talk to us. Draven texted me the details. They live in West Virginia, so it's not too far to travel. Sunny, that's their daughter, was at college in Seattle when the attack happened. Draven tracked down her old college roommate who ID'd Atwood after Draven showed her a photograph. According to her friend, Sunny met Atwood in a bar one night. They left together that evening, and we think that's when the attack must have happened. Sunny never returned to college."

"Did she…?" Christa bit her lip. "Did Sunny report it to the police, too?"

"We don't believe so. Draven couldn't find a case number. He's sent me the parents' contact details. They're willing to talk to us, so hopefully they can shed more light on what happened." I tucked a lock of hair behind her ear. "I think it would be a good idea if you came along, but I totally understand if you're not feeling up to it."

She shook her head firmly. "Nope. I'm coming. I feel much better than I did earlier in the week, and I want to hear what they've got to say. If I go, it personalizes it more, too. I want to offer my sympathies." She narrowed her eyes. "How long ago did she die?"

"Nine years."

She looked up and to the left, then cut her gaze back to me. "It happened after Kathy then."

"Yes."

"God, how many more?" She pressed her fingertips into her closed eyes and rubbed, her head shaking softly. "When I spoke to Kathy, she asked me why Sutton hadn't raped me. Why he'd sent someone else to do his dirty work." Her eyes watered. "I hadn't considered it, but why didn't he, Dayton? Why did I get off lightly, and yet these other girls—"

My eyebrows shot up. "Got off lightly? Are you kidding? Jesus, Christa, you almost died and nearly lost Max. Not to mention you were disfigured, scarred for life. That's not getting off lightly." I pulled her into my arms. "Angel, where is this coming from?"

She burrowed into my chest, almost as if she wanted to climb beneath my skin. "Maybe it was because we'd had a relationship, or maybe he just wanted me dead." She let out a shuddering breath. "I hate this, Dayton. I hate it so much. I just want it to be over. But it won't ever be over, will it?"

"Yes, it will." I kissed her hair. "We just have to dig in and keep going. Sooner or later that bastard is going to trip up. For all we know, Sunny could be the catalyst."

"That poor girl." She lifted herself, looking me squarely in the eye. "When are we going to see her parents?"

"Tomorrow. We'll fly down in the morning."

She sighed, then rose from the chair. "Mrs. Connor has left a casserole in the fridge. I'll heat it up, and after we've eaten, I think I'll go to bed."

I watched as she crossed over to the kitchen. This was definitely having an impact on her. Every interaction with Atwood stole a little more of her resolve, and being without Max tore her up. I had to find a way to end this, and quickly.

19

CHRISTA

"THANK you so much for seeing us, Mr. Pearson." I shook his outstretched hand, as did Dayton.

"You're welcome, my dear. Come on through to the kitchen. My wife has been baking cookies all morning." He lowered his voice. "They're not very tasty, but don't tell her I said that."

I grinned and followed him down a long, narrow hallway. Pictures adorned the walls of a fair-haired girl in various poses, but in each one, her smile was the first thing I noticed. Wide, bright, the kind that reached her eyes and made those she shared it with feel special.

"Is this Sunny?" I asked.

He nodded, pausing to scan the pictures. "Always smiling, that one. I swear she came out of her mom with a grin on her face." He winced. "She'd be twenty-eight now. Maybe married with a kiddo or two of her own."

"She looks so happy in these photos. We're terribly sorry, Mr. Pearson," Dayton said gently.

He nodded, then patted Dayton's arm. "Thank you, son."

We entered a large, airy kitchen with a big rustic table at the center. Mrs. Pearson was at the stove. She turned around, wiped her hands down her apron, and came toward us.

"You must be Dayton and Christa." We both received a warm hug. "Please have a seat. Would you like something to drink? I've baked cookies."

I caught Mr. Pearson's eye, and he put his finger to his lips and winked. God, these were such good people. They didn't deserve what had happened to them. My thoughts turned to Max, how it would break me to lose him. How difficult I'd find it to carry on if I couldn't hold my child in my arms, smell him, kiss him, shower him with love. How the Pearson's hadn't fractured under the death of their daughter humbled me. I would *not* allow Sunny's death to be in vain. Somehow, I'd find a way to take Sutton Atwood down.

"Coffee would be lovely, Mrs. Pearson," Dayton said.

Seemingly happy to have someone to fuss over, Mrs. Pearson bustled about the kitchen, pouring drinks and setting a large plate of cookies in the middle of the table. "There's plenty more where they came from, so don't be shy. Help yourselves."

I reached out and took a cookie, still warm from the oven. I nibbled on it. Contrary to Mr. Pearson's warning, they were pretty good, if a bit lacking in flavor.

"Delicious," I said, nudging Dayton.

He got my message and picked one up. He broke a piece off and ate it. I gathered it wasn't to his taste because he set the remainder next to his cup of coffee.

"Would you tell us what happened?" Dayton asked gently. "To Sunny."

Mrs. Pearson took a deep breath and reached out to clasp her husband's hand. Even after all this time, their pain and suffering was still very much present. Time hadn't eroded the agony of losing their only child.

"She was so excited about going off to college. The first in our family," Mr. Pearson said proudly. "Me and my brothers, we don't come from much, you see, but as soon as Sunny was born, we put away every cent we could for her future. And she didn't let us down, did she, love?"

Mrs. Pearson smiled. "No. She was a clever girl."

"What was she studying?" I asked.

"Psychology. She wanted to work with kids who'd suffered abuse." Mrs. Pearson stared off into space. "She was such a caring person, with a big heart."

Silence descended, each of them lost to their memories. Dayton opened his mouth to speak, but I shot him a look. The least we owed these people—who'd agreed to open old wounds for our benefit—was our patience.

Eventually, Mr. Pearson heaved a sigh. "She loved her first year. She'd call us every Sunday evening to tell us all her news, so excited at times, we couldn't even understand her. She came home for the summer and took a job at our local gas station. Then in the fall, she went back to Seattle."

He paused. I squeezed his arm. "Take your time."

"Four weeks before her nineteenth birthday, she turned up on our doorstep. I can still remember the shock when I opened the door. Her face was covered in bruises, and her eyes had this wildness about them. She threw herself at me, sobbing uncontrollably. It took three, no four, days until she told us what happened."

He glanced at his wife, and a silent conversation passed between them. Mrs. Pearson took over.

"She told us she'd been... raped." She squeezed her eyes closed, and a tear fell onto her cheek. "She'd taken herself to the hospital, but when they called the police, she checked herself out, got on a plane, and came home."

"She never reported it?" Dayton asked.

Mrs. Pearson shook her head. "I tried to persuade her, told her the man who'd done such a terrible thing shouldn't be allowed to get away with it, but she was adamant." Her watery gaze met mine. "She was terrified. Said he was a powerful man, and he'd threatened to kill her if she told anyone. I know my daughter, and she believed that threat one hundred percent.

"After that, she was never the same. She refused to go back to college. Instead, she locked herself in her room, rarely coming out. Then, a year to the day after he... after he..." Mrs. Pearson blew out a long, slow breath, her cheeks puffing out.

"You don't have to say it."

She glanced helplessly at her husband. He put his arm around her shoulders, hugging her to him.

"I went upstairs to ask her if she wanted something to eat," Mr. Pearson said. "It was a daily struggle, you know, getting food in her. Anyway, when she didn't answer, I opened the door and went inside. And I found her." He stared out of the window, his eyes taking on a distant look as though he was right back there, in that very moment, living the horror as it unfolded.

"I got her down, gave her CPR, but it was too late. She was gone."

He buried his face in his wife's hair, and the two of them began to quietly sob. I stared helplessly at Dayton who clutched my hand. After a few moments, they seemed to recover.

"When the man, Draven—he's a giant, isn't he? Sorry, I digress. When he came here and told us about you, miss, well I couldn't believe it, truth be told. I mean, a man like that... How does he get away with it?"

"He won't get away with it for much longer," Dayton growled. "Not if we have anything to do with it."

"Do you have a picture of Sunny? One you'd be willing to let me have?" I asked, an idea forming.

"Of course, love." Mr. Pearson got to his feet. He went over to the kitchen windowsill and picked up a photo frame. He removed the photograph and brought it over to me. It was of Sunny wearing a big floppy hat and a yellow sun dress, smiling into the camera. "I took that the summer she came home. That's how I like to remember her, not the shell of a girl she was at the end."

I slipped the photograph in my purse, taking care not to crease it. "Thank you so much. I'll make sure I return it."

"No need, love. I have it on my computer. I can easily print out another one."

Dayton and I stood, and I couldn't help going over to Mr. and Mrs. Pearson and giving them a hug. "Thank you so much for talking to us. I can't imagine how difficult that must have been."

Mr. Pearson patted my shoulder. "You take care of yourself, love. I hope we've helped."

"You have," Dayton said.

Mrs. Pearson insisted on wrapping up some cookies for us, and I didn't have the heart to stop her. Besides, it didn't do any harm to take them if it made her feel needed. Mr. Pearson saw us to the door.

"There's a trash can at the end of the street," he said, pointing his chin at the cookies.

I chuckled. "You're a little devil, aren't you, Mr. Pearson?"

He grinned. "You take care of this one now, son," he said to Dayton. "You hear me?"

"Yes, sir," Dayton replied. "She's safe with me."

Dayton settled me in the car then got in the driver's side. We waved to Mr. Pearson as Dayton pulled away from the curb.

"Why did you want the photograph?" he asked.

"Because we're going back to Seattle," I said. "I want to talk to Kathy."

Dayton glanced sideways at me before refocusing on the road. "You think what happened to Sunny will change her mind?"

I shrugged. "Only one way to find out."

20

DAYTON

WE LANDED in Seattle at three in the afternoon local time. It had already been a long day, and I worried about Christa. It had been less than two weeks since her surgery, and she'd had a lot to deal with during that time. A second weekend without Max, my father's funeral, flying around the country, her complete and utter refusal to take time off work. All of it had to be taking its toll, although to look at her, so strong, so determined, so beautiful, no one would guess there was any turmoil going on inside her. She'd crash at some point, and when she did, I'd be there to catch her. I'd never let her fall.

We taxied to a halt, and Christa unclipped her seat belt. "Let's do this," she said, rising to her feet.

"Hang on." I caught her hips and tugged her close. I skimmed my hand up her side, brushing my thumb over the curve of her breast, cupping her jaw. I bent my head and kissed her. It felt like forever since we'd connected sensually, and I missed her. I missed the feel of her soft lips on mine, the taste of her, the way she gasped when I pushed inside, our hot bodies sliding against one another. There'd been too much stress, too little time for us, and I didn't want to lose the closeness we'd created.

"Your timing sucks," she said, fisting my shirt as I drew back. "Hold that thought, okay? Because on the flight back, we're making use of the damned bedroom on this fancy plane of yours."

No, we wouldn't, not in the way she intimated, not until she was fully healed. But a little heavy petting, yep, *that* I would allow. "Fancy plane of *ours*," I said.

She rolled her eyes as she always did when I corrected her on the whole 'what's mine is yours' thing.

"Whatever. Now let's go and hope we can persuade Kathy to go to the police." She bit her lip. "I just hope we've got enough time. We have to be back for Max at six tomorrow."

"There's time," I said. "And if there isn't, we'll fly home, fetch Max, and fly back again."

She stood on tiptoes and pecked my lips. "You're pretty damned wonderful, you know that?"

"Don't tell my employees," I murmured against her mouth. "I like them thinking I'm a heartless bastard."

She chuckled, then fluttered her eyelashes. "Whatever you say, *sir*."

I groaned, loving these moments of light, of intimacy, even if we were living in the middle of a nightmare. "Fuck, woman. Don't do *that* to me."

She playfully bumped my shoulder, then fit her small hand inside my much larger one. "Let's go. I just hope Kathy is on shift tonight."

We arrived at the restaurant where Kathy worked at five after four. The same woman, Marsha, was standing behind the podium serving a couple and their three kids. She caught my eye and raised her eyebrows in recognition.

"This way," she said to the family, glancing back over her shoulder. "Take a seat. I'll be right with you."

We remained standing. I scanned the restaurant looking for Kathy, spotting her on the far side, taking an order. I nudged Christa, then pointed with my chin. "We're in luck."

She tracked my gaze, then set off. I followed. Clearly, we weren't waiting for Marsha to return.

"Kathy," Christa quietly called out as we approached her.

Kathy's head spun around, and her eyes widened. "Wh-what are you doing back here?" She brushed past us on her way to her station. "I can't talk now. I'm working."

"You're not the only one he attacked," Christa said to her retreating form.

Kathy skidded to a halt, paused, then slowly turned around, dismay etched on her face. "There's another girl? Here?"

"No. She's dead," Christa said bluntly. "She hung herself because she couldn't live with what he'd done to her. He attacked her two years after he attacked you."

Kathy's hand covered her mouth, and she paled. "Oh God," she croaked.

"Exactly. How many more could there be, Kathy? Are you really willing to stand by and let him get away with this?" She slipped her hand into her purse and pulled out Sunny's picture, holding it in front of Kathy's face. "This is her. Sunny Pearson. She was nineteen years old. She had her whole life ahead of her, but he stole it." She closed the distance between them and touched Kathy's arm. "He stole from her, and you, and me, and God only knows how many more. Please, Kathy. I'm begging you. Help me stop him."

My chest swelled with pride. What a woman. *My* woman.

Kathy stared at Sunny's picture for the longest time. Her eyes closed briefly, and her bottom lip wobbled as though she was going to cry. When she opened her eyes, they were brimful of tears and, one by one, they fell onto her cheeks.

"I'm so scared," she whispered.

Christa's arms went around her, and she held her tightly. "I know, Kathy. It's okay."

I went to find the manager, explained we were friends of Kathy's and that she wasn't well, and we were taking her home. He wasn't happy, but I didn't give a shit, and I told him precisely that. My body language, the glare I hit him with, and the jut of my jaw dared him to argue with me.

He took the sensible option.

"We're out of here," I said, touching Christa's shoulder. "Come on, Kathy."

"M-my job—"

"It's fine. I've squared it with your manager."

I placed the palm of my hand on Christa's lower back and edged her toward the door. She captured Kathy's hand, and we left. I drove us to a nearby hotel that I knew had a quiet lobby bar, somewhere we'd be able to talk in private. Kathy shivered when we got out of the car, despite the warmth of the late afternoon sunshine. I think her chill was more to do with the dawning realization that if she'd stuck to her guns and pressed charges, Atwood might have been put away. If he'd been in prison, he wouldn't have been able to attack Sunny.

That wasn't altogether a fair assumption. For all we knew, Kathy hadn't been the first. There could be countless victims out there. I shuddered at such a horrific thought.

I invited over the bartender and gave him our drinks order. While I waited for him to return, I stepped away to check my phone, leaving Christa to try to calm Kathy. She'd probably have more luck without me crowding them.

I made a quick call to Draven to update him and to check on Max. With any luck, Atwood's days were numbered, both in terms of being able to see Max, and as a free man. I wouldn't stop looking until I'd found every single woman he'd abused, and I'd make sure the police added each one to that bastard's rap sheet. If I had my way, that fucker would be carried out of prison in a body bag.

I returned to our table. Christa and Kathy were deep in conversation. I slid onto my seat and picked up my whiskey, knocking it back in one go.

"I just spoke to Draven," I said to Christa. "Max is okay."

She reached across the table and squeezed my hand. "Thank you for checking."

I nodded. "So, how we doing?"

Kathy met my gaze. "I want to help, Mr. Somers. Really, I do. But I'm terrified what he'll do to me, or worse, to my daughter. He has the power to take her from me, just like he's doing with your son. I can't risk that. I'm so sorry, but I can't help you."

Same old excuses, and I'd had enough. I was going to push this woman into doing the right thing. Yes, that made me a heartless bastard, but my main concern, my *only* concern was Christa and Max.

I laced my fingers, then rested my hands on the table. "Here's what's going to happen. We're going to finish our drinks and then Christa is going to call her friend, Detective Harris." Kathy opened her mouth to interrupt. I shot her a stern glare that dared her to utter a single word until I'd finished. She clamped her mouth shut.

"We're going to make arrangements for him to take your statement about what Atwood put you through. Christa will be by your side the entire time. And after you've made your statement, you and your daughter are coming back to New York with us. I own another apartment in the building I live in. You can stay there, rent free, for as long as it takes to put Atwood away for good. Then, if you choose to return to Seattle, fine. If you want to stay, also fine. We'll come to an arrangement over the apartment. While that fucker is walking the streets, I will provide you with as much protection as it takes to make you feel safe.

Round the clock if that's what you want. And when it's all over, when you're ready, I'll give you a job and arrange schooling for your daughter. But I'll tell you what isn't going to happen." I edged closer, my gaze locked on hers. She rapidly blinked. "You are *not* going to let him get away with this. You *will* make a statement. No arguments."

"Dayton," Christa began, but I silenced her with a look, then turned my attention back to Kathy.

"Ready?" I asked, getting to my feet.

She swallowed and wrapped her arms around her body. Taking a deep breath, Kathy tipped her head back and slowly nodded, a determined expression on her face.

"I'm ready."

21

CHRISTA

I SPOTTED Detective George Harris standing outside the police department. He gave me a bright grin and a wave. I felt the nervous tension rolling off Kathy, and her breathing came out low and shallow.

"It's going to be fine," I said in what I hoped was a reassuring tone. I took hold of her hand and gave it a squeeze. "George is wonderful, and I'll be with you the whole time."

She didn't respond, but she did increase the pressure on my hand, a silent message that I read as a thank you.

"George," I said, releasing Kathy's hand to give him a hug. "You look wonderful. How are you doing?"

"Well, I've got a little less hair and a little more gut since I last saw you," he said, rubbing his stomach. "But I can't complain." He held out his hand to Kathy. "Nice to meet you, Ms. Johnson."

"And you," she said quietly.

"Thanks for seeing us on a Sunday, George." It wasn't yet eight in the morning, but Dayton and I had to be back in New York by five at the latest. Any later and we risked being late for Max. That could not happen.

"Not a problem. Please, follow me. I've arranged a room where we can talk privately."

He showed us to a windowless room with a table that had four metal chairs around it, all pushed underneath. George settled us in then went to get drinks, returning with three plastic cups brim-full of coffee from a vending machine. I took a sip, then wrinkled my nose.

"I know. Tastes like crap," George said, grinning. "Still, it's wet and hot, as my mother would say."

"What's going to happen?" Kathy asked quietly, clenching then unclenching her hands.

George gave her a friendly smile. I was so glad he had the time to conduct this interview, because I wouldn't have wanted to risk Kathy's trust in me to anyone else.

"I'll ask you a few questions, just to get the ball rolling, but I'll be led completely by you. There are no expectations, Ms. Johnson. You go at your own pace."

"Will I be recorded?" she asked, glancing nervously at the tape machine on the edge of the table.

"Yes, if that's okay?"

She shrugged. "I guess."

George set up the tape, and once he was satisfied, he turned his attention to Kathy. "Why don't you start by telling me how you first met Sutton Atwood."

As I listened to Kathy haltingly tell her story, a hard knot formed in my stomach. I, more than most, knew how rotten Sutton was, how sadistic and brutal he could be, but hearing firsthand what he'd done to the woman sitting beside me, brought my own horrors crashing back. And this was the man who, right this second, had custody of my son. The only reason I managed to hold it together was because of the measures Dayton had put in place. I'd have gone crazy had I not known that Draven and his team were watching over Max. With any luck, Kathy's courageous stand would not only bring her closure—as well as the ability to finally move on with her life—but would also allow me to free Max from the clutches of a madman.

George listened attentively, occasionally interrupting to ask an additional question or to delve a little deeper, but in the main, he simply sat there, hands resting in his lap. His face was devoid of emotion, but I knew George. Being a detective for thirty years might mean he'd seen and heard it all, but that didn't mean he'd stopped caring. He'd demonstrated the depth of his empathy with the way he'd shown such concern and consideration for me during the two years after my own assault.

An hour later, Kathy took a deep, shuddering breath, then let it out slowly through pursed lips. She turned to me, her eyes glistening with unshed tears. "Thank you."

I raised my eyebrows. "What for?"

"For encouraging me to do this. For being by my side the whole time. I feel… free. I mean, I'm still terrified what he'll do when he finds out I've gone to the police, but just telling my story… having people believe me. It means a lot."

I rubbed her upper arm. "You're welcome."

I refrained from reminding her that Dayton hadn't really given her a choice and, although his move had been a risky one, it had paid off. Then again, Dayton was used to taking calculated risks. He'd behaved in an extremely assertive manner with Kathy, but I got the impression his forceful demand had been exactly what she'd needed to give her a push in the right direction, not only to do the right thing, but also to wrestle free from Sutton's hold over her.

"What happens now?" she asked George.

"We'll bring him in for questioning as soon as he returns to Seattle."

I'd updated George as to Sutton's current whereabouts.

"The fact that we have your initial complaint on record is helpful," George said. "And we still have the DNA from that time as well as the pictures the hospital took."

I shook my head. "What I don't understand, George, is why charges weren't brought in spite of Kathy's refusal to make a statement. Surely there was enough without that to charge him?"

George twisted his lips to one side. "Without Kathy's testimony, Atwood was able to freely claim the sex was consensual. I've read the interview notes, and he insisted she liked it rough."

Kathy winced.

"Total bullshit," I said, angry on Kathy's behalf, and Sunny's, and anyone else Sutton had robbed of their lives through his vile and savage actions. "What, rough enough to end up in the hospital with unspeakable injuries?"

George hitched a shoulder. "Believe it or not, there are women, and men, out there who get off on precisely that. That's why the case collapsed once the statement was recanted."

"I'm so sorry," Kathy whispered, her tears finally falling. "If I'd been braver, then Sunny wouldn't have been raped, and she'd still be alive."

I put my arm around her shoulder, while George said, "You don't know that. Even with your testimony, there would have been no guarantees of a conviction."

I shot him a grateful smile. The very last thing Kathy needed was to take the blame for what happened to Sunny. She carried enough guilt as it was.

We rose to leave, but George indicated for me to stay back. I opened the door to let Kathy out and told her I'd catch up with her shortly.

"What's up?"

He pointed to the chair I'd vacated. "Have a seat."

I pulled it out, the metal scraping on the cheap flooring. "You really should get some cushioning on these seats, George," I said, wincing as I sat. "They're really uncomfortable."

"Try sitting on them all day, every day," he said. "Budgets don't stretch to comfort, I'm afraid."

I grinned. "I'll have some cushions couriered over, just for you."

George didn't return my smile. "Christa, listen. When we bring Atwood in for questioning, it's going to set off a chain reaction. He's not stupid. He's gotten away with this for years, and he'll know you've had something to do with Kathy coming forward after all this time. I worry for you, and for Kathy."

Fear took root in my stomach, but I refused to give in to it. Sutton deserved everything coming his way. I wanted him to suffer, to know what it felt like to be terrified, to pay for his crimes.

"I'm aware of the risks, George. Kathy and her daughter are coming back to New York with us. Dayton is arranging a place for them to stay, and he'll have security assigned to them, and no doubt, to me, too. I won't take any chances, I promise."

"Make sure you don't," he said gruffly, clearing his throat.

I got up and walked around the table so I could hug him. "You've been a wonderful friend to me, George, and I know you'll do right by Kathy. Help us get him, please."

"I'll do everything in my power." He looked up at me with something akin to pride in his eyes. "You always were strong, Christa, but now, you're tough as well. And you'll need to be, because you're in for a very bumpy ride."

I nodded. "I'm ready, George. With Dayton by my side, I'm ready for anything Sutton throws at me."

22

DAYTON

"STEP ON IT, PAUL," I ordered. Beside me, Christa fidgeted, as worried as I was that we'd be late back for Max. There'd been a delay because of some issue with air traffic control, and we'd landed an hour later than planned. Kathy and her daughter were sitting opposite, their eyes wide, in awe of the opulence of the limo's interior. I'd been rich for so long, I often forgot that it could be overwhelming for those not used to it.

Wait until they saw the apartment. I'd spent the time this morning—while Kathy and Christa had been at the police station —making various phone calls. The previous owner hadn't left any furniture, and because there wasn't time to set up the entire place, I—or rather Angie—had pulled a few strings and arranged for a couple of couches and beds to be delivered.

"Wreck up ahead, sir," Paul said.

"Fuck!" I expelled, then, remembering there was a kid in the car, I shot an apologetic glance at Kathy. "Sorry."

She smiled. "Given what you're doing for us, Mr. Somers, I'd say you can cuss as much as you like."

A warm feeling spread through my chest. *Jesus. I'm getting soft in my old age.*

"I'll get off the freeway," Paul said, taking the last exit as cars started braking ahead. "Take our chances on the minor roads."

"We're not going to make it, are we?" Christa asked, panic seeping into her tone. "He'll use that against us. And what about Kathy? We can't let him see her."

I captured Christa's hand and brought it to my lips. "Easy, angel. We'll make it. And he won't see Kathy. He can't get access to the penthouse, so he'll have to wait in the lobby, and Paul will drive straight into the garage. Relax. Everything is under control."

I glanced at my watch. Thirty minutes until Atwood was due to drop Max off. We were cutting it close, but I trusted in Paul's skill behind the wheel. He was breaking every speed limit—if the speed of the landscape passing us by was anything to go by.

We turned into my underground garage with five minutes to spare. My heart pounded as I flung open the door before Paul had fully stopped the car. He braked hard, still halfway out of the parking space.

"Come on," I said, taking Christa's hand and making sure Kathy and her daughter were right behind us. I ushered them all into the elevator and punched in the code. I opened the door to my penthouse.

Kathy's eyes widened when she walked inside, and her daughter exclaimed, "Wow!"

My phone buzzed, the receptionist letting me know Atwood had arrived in the lobby. She wouldn't let him up without my specific permission, which I reluctantly gave. There were only two codes for my private elevator: the one Christa and I had, as well as Nina, and the one held by reception. The latter could only be used with sanction from either me or Christa.

"He's here," I said. "Christa, take Kathy and Tilly upstairs to the library then get back down here quick as you can."

"Okay." She disappeared with Kathy and her daughter in tow.

I walked to the entranceway and waited by the elevator. It pinged the second I got there. *Too close for comfort.*

Atwood appeared, Max by his side. As Max went to run toward me, Atwood clasped his shoulder, stopping him.

"Where's Christa?"

"She's upstairs. She'll be down in a second." I crouched and held my arms out to Max. "Come on, bud."

Max wriggled free and threw himself at me. "Dada."

A flash of anger crossed Atwood's face. "No, Max," he said through gritted teeth. "We've talked about this. *I'm* your dada."

I'm going to fucking kill him.

Max's brow furrowed in confusion. He glanced over his shoulder at Atwood then back at me. He bent his head over to the left. "Dada?"

"I said—"

"We heard what you said, Sutton." Christa appeared behind me, her jaw clenched tightly, a flush of red mottling her neck. "Hi, baby." She lifted Max out of my arms and swung him high into the air, then covered his face with kisses. "Have you had a good time?"

He nodded, giggling. "Yep."

I smiled at Max's customary affirmative response and slipped my arm around Christa's waist. With a blank stare at Atwood, I said, "You can go now."

His eyes flashed with unadulterated hatred. He pointed his finger at Christa. "You tell him the fucking truth, or I'm gonna lose my shit."

Okay, now I've had enough. My hands automatically made a fist. "Christa, go inside," I demanded.

Without a murmur of dissent, she went, holding Max tightly to her. I waited until the door clicked shut behind me. In two steps, I reached Atwood. I gripped him around the throat. I shouldn't have done it, but as there weren't any witnesses, what the fuck was he gonna do? His eyes bugged, and he grabbed my wrists, trying to tug my hand away. I squeezed harder.

"You listen to me, you fucking animal. *I'm* gonna lose *my* shit if you don't rein in your mouth. You feel me?" I slammed him hard against the wall. His head made a dull thud as it connected with the drywall. "Don't fucking push me, because you have *no* idea what I'm capable of."

I let him go, and he gasped for air. "You just made a big fucking mistake," he wheezed, rubbing at his throat.

I laughed. "I beg to differ. Most fun I've had in a while." I jerked my chin at the elevator. "Now get the fuck off my property."

I stood with my legs wide, my arms loose by my sides. I wanted him to take a swing, and I wanted the punch to land, because it would give me an excuse to hit back. And hell, I wanted to hit back, really fucking badly. Unfortunately, Atwood might be a lot of things, but idiotic wasn't one of them. Despite the venom shooting from his eyes and the clenched fists that told me he was tempted, he knew as well as I did that hitting me would only play into my hands.

"She'd better tell Max I'm his father," he said through gritted teeth.

I arched an eyebrow and drawled, "Or?"

"Keep up this bullshit, and you'll find out."

You are so full of crap, dickhead. I rolled my eyes and yawned, then crossed to the elevator and jabbed a finger at the call button. The doors opened immediately. "Get out."

He rammed me with his shoulder as he passed. I stood firm. The doors started to close, but then his foot appeared between them, and they sprang back open.

"Oh, I forgot to mention," he said, a smug grin on his face. "As things are going so well with Max, my solicitor has recommended the time is right to apply for more permanent custody.

He reckons the judge will grant at least a fifty-fifty arrangement. See you in court, buddy."

The doors closed, and he disappeared.

A knot formed in my stomach, and I pinched the bridge of my nose as my temper raged. George and his coworkers in the Seattle police force had better get the mud to stick to that bastard —otherwise we were in deep trouble.

23

CHRISTA

"WHAT TIME IS IT?" I asked for the umpteenth time.

"Five minutes after the last time you asked," Dayton replied, his hand reaching for mine as we traveled to the office in the back of his limo. I'd barely slept knowing that today was the day Sutton would be hauled in for questioning. I had no idea what his reaction would be, but George's warning reverberated around my head. He'd go ballistic, I knew that. And I was ready, or at least I thought I was ready, for him to use his special brand of retribution—Max.

Dayton had repeated what Sutton had said to him, that he was applying for shared custody. We'd updated Francesca last night, and she'd asked us to keep her posted. She did confirm, however, that if the police charged him with Kathy's rape and assault, then Francesca would apply for—and likely win—immediate cessation of all contact that Sutton had been granted, at least until Kathy's case came to court and was concluded.

I just had to hope and pray that there'd be enough evidence to put him away for a real long stretch. Although I'd thought that after my own torturous trip through the court system. I'd assumed that when the jury came back with the guilty verdict, my nightmare was over. Little did I know, it was only just beginning. And I had no doubt Sutton would grease a few more palms to try to wriggle out of the latest allegations heading his way. But we had to give it a shot. Quitting wasn't an option.

"Try not to worry," Dayton said.

I grimaced. "Easier said than done."

"I know, but there's nothing you can do until George calls. Did he give you any indication of when that might be?"

I shook my head, wrestling the empty bag of grapes from Max's clenched fist. I removed a wipe from my purse and cleaned his sticky fingers.

"Well, Draven texted me to confirm Atwood arrived back in Seattle at three this morning. I'd guess, given the seriousness of the allegations, they'd want to pick him up as soon as possible."

"The waiting is the hardest." I nibbled the skin around my thumbnail until Dayton tugged my hand away from my face. "I should imagine Kathy is equally on edge. Just knowing he'd been so close to her last night was enough to send the poor woman into a panic."

"She'll be fine in the apartment. She knows not to answer the door to anyone until her security detail arrives later today. I'm going to speak to Draven about getting a detail put on you, too, whenever I'm not around. I want reassurance you're both safe until that f—" He glanced at Max. "Until all this is behind us."

I nodded. I wasn't going to fight him on this. I had too much self-preservation to take any risks.

Dayton and I parted company in the lobby. I promised to call him as soon as George made contact. After dropping off Max at childcare, I headed up to my office, knowing my productivity was going to be shot today. My mind wouldn't stop racing in a million different directions, and concentrating on programming code required focus and discipline.

It was after three in the afternoon before my phone dinged with a text, and the sender showed as 'George.' My heart galloped, and my palms dampened so quickly, I dropped my phone twice. On the third attempt, I managed to swipe the screen and open the text.

Call me.

Shit. I scrambled from my chair, muttering under my breath. Several of my coworkers looked up from their computers. I dashed out of the office and ducked into an empty conference room. My hands shook as I pressed call. The sound of blood rushed through my ears, even louder than when Dayton and I had gone to Niagara Falls.

"George," I said the second he answered. "What news?"

"Hi, Christa. Thanks for getting back to me. We questioned Atwood this morning. He's denied it all, of course. As expected, his defense was that the sex with Kathy was consensual. He contested knowing Sunny, and without any evidence to the contrary, we can't refute that, but with Kathy, we have the DNA evidence from the time of the assault, as well as her statement."

"You've charged him?"

"Not yet."

My stomach lurched, and, as my knees wobbled, I gripped the back of a chair. "Why not?"

"Because we're still putting the case together. These things take time, Christa. You, of all people, should know that."

"My case took two years to come to fruition, George. Please tell me this one isn't going to be a repeat performance."

"I certainly hope not." He paused. "Promise me you'll arrange for some personal protection."

I brushed a hand over my face and expelled a deep sigh. "He knows it was me?"

"We didn't let on, of course, but yeah, I'd say he knows you're behind it."

It wasn't unexpected, but even so, anxiety clawed at my gut, and a creeping sense of unease weighed me down. I wasn't ashamed to admit that Sutton terrified me, even more so since meeting Kathy, and Sunny's parents. Sutton's crimes were far more reaching than I'd ever imagined. He had a black heart, and I had no doubt he'd stoop to any lengths in order to save himself.

"Keep me posted, yeah, George?"

"Of course."

I cut the call and dashed straight up to Dayton's office. I had to cool my heels waiting outside because he was in the middle of a board meeting and, as important as this was, I didn't want to interrupt his work. He'd missed enough time at the office these last few weeks. Telling him Sutton had been questioned could wait until Dayton had finished. It wasn't like I expected Sutton to burst in here and drag me off, kicking and screaming. No, he'd be much more subtle. Besides, he was in Seattle. Even he hadn't figured out how to be in two places at once.

The door to Dayton's office opened, and his senior management team filed out, one by one. As soon as the last one exited, Angie gave me the nod to enter.

I slipped inside and closed the door. Dayton had his head buried in a stack of papers, his ankle crossed over his knee, pen in hand, scribbling notes.

"George called."

His head snapped up. He dropped the papers on the table and got to his feet. "What did he say?"

I threw myself at him, nestling in tight. Dayton made me feel safe, protected, secure, and I was desperate for reassurance.

"Angel." He stroked my hair, allowing me the comfort I needed. After a few moments, he eased me back. "Tell me."

"There isn't much to tell. Sutton denied it all, which we knew he would. They've let him go for now while they carry out further inquiries." I bit my lip. "I hoped they'd lock him up right away."

Dayton kissed my forehead. "Me, too."

"He knows we set this in motion."

He twisted his lips in a wry fashion. "We anticipated that."

"I'm scared."

"Oh, angel." He put his arms around me once more. "I promise nothing is going to happen to you. He'll know the police are watching and that we're on our guard. I've said this before. He's evil, not stupid."

My head bobbed against his chest, and I soaked up his warmth. "I'm so lucky to have you."

He curled a finger under my chin and tilted my head up until I met his loving gaze. "Ditto."

―――――

I expected Sutton to call me, to let off steam with some vitriolic diatribe, but I should have known by now to always expect the unexpected when it came to him. My phone remained eerily silent. Instead of easing my anxiety, though, the absence of any form of contact intensified my fear.

Wednesday arrived—Sutton's day to have Max—but he didn't turn up. According to Draven, he'd remained in Seattle and was showing no sign of getting on a plane to New York. Dayton called Francesca to report the no-show, and she promised to inform the judge. I had no idea whether this would result in a strike against Sutton, but surely it had to be a positive in our favor?

Kathy and her daughter had settled in well. Dayton not only arranged for round-the-clock security for them, but also home-schooling for Tilly after Kathy was reluctant to allow her daughter to attend school until Sutton was behind bars. I understood, and concurred with, her concerns.

It was Thursday evening when Francesca called to tell us that Sutton had contacted the court with some bullshit story that a family member was ill, hence the reason why he hadn't been able to pick up Max, but that he intended on keeping to next week's schedule.

"Probably too busy trying to keep his ass out of jail," Dayton said.

I hoped he failed in that mission.

"It's Max's birthday on Saturday," I said. "I know we've been stressed and busy, but I don't want it to simply pass by."

Dayton grinned. "It won't."

I sat up straight, frowning. "What did you have in mind?"

"Well," he said, drawing out the word to increase my anticipation. I dug him in the ribs, and he fake-groaned. "I may have booked out the Stardust Diner and arranged for all his friends from daycare to attend."

My heart squeezed. This guy... The Stardust Diner had been where we'd kind of had our first date. Well, not our first date exactly. It had been the place where we'd connected, and I'd started to see Dayton as one of the good guys rather than a powerful, arrogant man who reminded me of Sutton.

Tears filled my eyes. "You're the best," I said through snivels and blurred vision.

He blew on the tips of his fingers. "I know."

24

CHRISTA

"AND THAT'S why we think this particular application is perfect for your needs." I smiled at the sea of faces all directed at me. "Any questions?"

I fielded a couple with ease, then closed down the presentation. Greg gave me the tiniest of nods. *Yes!* He was happy. Considering my mind was all over the place at the moment, I couldn't be more thrilled it had gone well. Now we just needed them to sign on the dotted line and I'd have landed my first big client.

"So, ladies, gents, let's talk next steps."

A soft knock on the door of the conference room drew my attention.

Greg's PA stuck her head around the door. "I'm so sorry to interrupt. Christa, could I have a quick word?"

My stomach flipped over. *Wonder what the problem is?* It couldn't be good if she'd thought it necessary to interrupt an important meeting at such a crucial time. "Of course. Excuse me." I followed her outside, closing the door quietly behind me. "What's up?"

"Sondra has called from the childcare center. Max isn't

well."

"What's wrong?" I asked, panicked.

She touched my arm. "I think it's just a tummy bug. Nothing to worry about."

"Oh." I clasped a hand to my chest. "Kids. It's easy to jump to conclusions and think the worst. He probably picked up something at his birthday party on Saturday or ate too much cake."

She grinned. "Yeah, they never know when to stop with the sweet stuff."

"Thanks for coming to let me know. I'll make my apologies and then go pick him up."

I popped back inside the conference room. "I'm so sorry, but I've just been informed my little boy isn't feeling well. I'll be back online within the hour if you have any further questions."

"Thank you, Ms. Adams," Simon, the lead negotiator said, standing to shake my hand. "I'll be in touch. I hope your son is feeling better soon."

Greg walked me out, his grin broad the second he'd closed the door. "Well done. You rocked it in there. Now go get Max. Hope it's nothing too serious."

"Thanks. I'll call you."

I strode to the elevator and pressed the button for the basement. Despite Max being unwell, I couldn't stop smiling. This professional boost was just what I needed to raise my spirits. It was almost a year since I'd joined Dayton's firm, and I loved working here more than ever.

When I walked inside the childcare center, I spotted Sondra sitting on a couch rocking Max in her lap. He was sucking his thumb, something he hadn't done for a while now. I jogged across, crouching to his level. I brushed his hair off his forehead. His skin was clammy, and he definitely had a temperature. "Hey, little man. You not feeling so good?"

He shook his head.

"Probably a virus," Sondra said, handing him to me. "I've

given him some cold medicine, but I think what he really needs is his mommy and his bed."

"Thanks, Sondra." I cradled him to me. "Come on, let's get you home."

I called Dayton, but his phone went to voicemail. I left a message then called Paul to come pick us up as per Dayton's instructions. No cabs, no subways, no traveling anywhere alone until Sutton was off the streets. If that didn't happen, I wasn't sure what our next move would be, but until we knew for definite whether Sutton would be charged for his crimes, I wasn't going to argue with Dayton.

I only had to wait in the lobby for a minute or so before Paul drove up outside.

"Thanks for coming so quickly," I said.

"It's my job, miss," Paul replied seriously.

My lips twitched. Paul didn't come across as the friendliest, but that was because he was the consummate professional and a fantastic employee.

I strapped Max in his car seat then climbed in the back. Paul filtered into the busy traffic, and I let my head fall back against the seat. My phone vibrated, and I took it out of my bag. Dayton.

"I got a missed call," he said. "You okay?"

"Yeah. Max isn't well. I'm on my way home with him."

"What's the matter?" Worry bled through his tone.

"Nothing to be concerned about. I think it's a bug of some sort. He'll be fine in a day or two. The presentation went great, by the way."

"I never had any doubt," Dayton replied. "I'm proud of you."

A great big goofy grin planted itself on my face. Dayton's approval was something I craved. He was so damned good at what he did, I always worried I'd let him down

"Thank you. That means a lot."

"You're in the car with Paul, right?"

"Of course," I said patiently. *As if I'd dare not be.*

"Put me on speakerphone."

"Why?"

"Just do it, Christa."

I huffed a breath then did as he'd asked.

"Paul, I want you to make sure you escort Ms. Adams and Max up to the apartment. You see her right inside, yes?"

I met Paul's gaze in the rearview mirror and rolled my eyes. I swear one corner of his mouth turned upward.

"Yes, sir."

"Good. Christa, call me as soon as you get home."

"I will. Bye." I hung up. "Jeez, what a worry wart."

"Better to be safe than sorry, miss," Paul said.

God, they were like a pair of bookends. I turned my attention to Max. His eyes were closed, and his breathing heavy. Poor little guy had fallen asleep. I felt his forehead again. Still warm, but not overly so. No need to call the doctor.

Paul pulled into the garage and, as he'd promised, traveled in the elevator up to the apartment. "Lock this door behind me, miss," he said.

I did as instructed. Mrs. Connor was in the kitchen preparing our dinner for that evening. I didn't see her very much as she worked part-time during the day.

"Something smells good, Mrs. C," I said.

She looked up as she heard my voice. "Oh, Christa, you're home early." She frowned as she spotted Max with his head on my shoulder. "What's the matter? Is Max unwell?"

I nodded. "He's feeling under the weather. I'm going to put him to bed and then get some work done."

"I'm almost finished here, and then I'll get out of your way," she said.

I went to my study, called Dayton, then answered a few emails, but when nothing urgent caught my attention, I shut down my computer. I wandered back into the living area. Mrs. C had left for the day. There was a casserole bubbling on the stove.

God bless the woman. I wasn't a bad cook, but Mrs. C was an *amazing* cook. Not for the first time, I wondered how on earth I'd ended up in a long-term relationship with a super-hot, kind and generous billionaire, and a life that offered such privilege.

The only blip on the radar was my continued battle with Sutton. Why hadn't he been in contact? What was he up to? Whatever his plans were, causing me the maximum amount of pain and anguish would be his number one priority. The thing was, he'd achieved that simply through his silence because as each day passed without some form of retribution, the more my fear grew.

I checked on Max who was fast asleep. Dayton wouldn't be home for a couple of hours, and boredom had set in. There was nothing that needed cleaning, or tidying, no groceries to pick up, no ironing to do.

And then a thought occurred to me. It felt like ages since we'd connected as a couple. An image popped into my mind. Candlelight, soft music, a bottle of wine, Mrs. C's delicious casserole. With renewed vigor, I strode down the hallway to our bedroom and jumped in the shower.

Mr. Somers, prepare to be seduced.

A shiver of anticipation crept up my spine as I washed, waxed, buffed, and moisturized my entire body. I sat at my dresser and dried my hair, leaving it loose, its natural waviness cascading down my back. I added a touch of light makeup and then entered the walk-in closet. I riffled through, my gaze eventually falling on a dress I'd bought a few weeks ago. It was very revealing and not something I'd be brave enough to wear in public. But privately? A whole different story.

I slipped it on and checked myself out in the floor-to-ceiling mirror. Oh yeah. Dayton wouldn't be able to resist. Take a back seat, fuck-me heels, 'cause this was a fuck-me dress if ever I saw one.

I padded down the hallway, grinning. I probably had an hour

to kill. If Mrs. C hadn't made a dessert, I might rustle up some baked caramel apples with lots of cinnamon—a favorite of Dayton's.

I walked into the living room—and froze.

Sitting on the couch, a huge teddy bear and a bunch of balloons by his side, was Sutton.

And he had a gun pointed right at me.

25

CHRISTA

"WH-WHAT ARE YOU DOING?"

Sutton's lips curled into a cruel smile, one I knew well. He tapped the barrel of the gun on the spare seat beside him.

"Sit."

I wasn't sure my legs would carry me. They felt weak as jelly, like all the bones had been removed. I put one foot forward, my thighs trembling.

"How did you get in here?"

He grabbed the teddy bear by the arm and shook it. "Amazing what a bit of charm and a stuffed toy can do. Your receptionist couldn't let me up here fast enough when I laid it on that I missed my son's birthday on Saturday—my *only* son's fucking birthday—and how I wanted to bring him some gifts. She was like mush in my hands. Stupid bitch."

Oh God. There'd been a couple of temps on the reception desk recently because of a particularly nasty virus going around. The staff member who'd let Sutton up here must have been one of them. She mustn't be familiar with protocol.

Shit, shit, shit. Think, Christa.

I took another step but clearly wasn't moving fast enough for Sutton because he cocked the gun. "Sit the fuck down, Sienna."

The reversion to my former name was a purposeful move. It sent the message that Sutton was in charge, that I was his puppet to play with. I willed my legs to move faster, virtually falling into the chair opposite.

"Oh no," he said, tossing the teddy bear to one side. Once again, he tapped the seat next to his with the gun. "Sit right here."

My mouth dried up, my heart thumped, and the sound of my blood rushed through my ears. I somehow struggled to my feet and crossed over to him. I couldn't take my eyes off the gun. I'd never seen a firearm up close, but I doubted it was fake.

Oh God. I could die tonight. Max could die tonight.

"What do you want, Sutton?"

He grabbed a fistful of my hair and yanked, hard.

I cried out, tears springing to my eyes.

"Where is she?" he bit out.

"Where's who?"

He pulled again, tearing a chunk of my hair out at the roots. I screamed in pain.

"Don't test me, Sienna. Where. Is. That. Fucking. Slut. Kathy."

He yelled each word in my face, spittle forming in the corner of his mouth, the odd bit splattering on my face.

"I don't know," I said. "Honestly, Sutton, I don't know where she is."

"You're lying!" He jabbed the barrel of the gun into my temple. "Don't lie to me, goddammit."

My entire body shook, and I took shallow, gasping breaths. Fear rendered me absolutely paralyzed. *Please, God, just let Max live. Let my little boy survive.*

"Where is she?"

"Please, Sutton. Don't hurt me. Think of Max. He needs his mommy. Please."

He barked out a laugh, the sound sending fear racing through my veins. He pressed the gun even harder against my head. "You mean the kid that shouldn't even be here if you'd done as you were fucking told and got rid of it. Like I told you to. Like you were supposed to!"

Saliva filled my mouth, nausea swirling in the pit of my stomach. I was trapped with a madman. A sick, sick man who couldn't possibly have normal feelings because he was certifiably insane. I'd been lulled into thinking he might have grown to care about Max during the time he'd spent with him, but he didn't care at all. The only thing Sutton Atwood gave a shit about was himself and his revenge. Terror for my son rendered me speechless. All the bravery in the world was meaningless when you had a gun to your head. One false move, and Sutton would pull the trigger. I had absolutely no doubt. Desperate men did desperate things. And Sutton showed all the signs of being desperate.

Oh God, Dayton.

He'd be home at any minute, and there was no way for me to warn him. I had to find a way to disarm Sutton, or at the very least, keep him off balance while I tried to come up with something that would keep everyone I cared about safe.

Max, Dayton, Kathy, and her daughter. They all needed me to hold it together and think of a solution to this situation. The only thing that might buy me some time was contrition. If I pretended I was sorry, kept Sutton talking, maybe, just maybe, that would work.

Max, I love you more than my own life. Please forgive me for what I am about to say.

"You were right, Sutton. I should have listened to you. Having a kid ruined everything. I should have done as I was told. If I had, we'd still be together."

His eyes narrowed, and for a split second, I thought he believed me. Stupid, stupid me. His lips thinned, and he sneered.

"Nice try, babe."

He smashed the butt of the gun against my temple. Agonizing pain shot through my head, the room spun, and then I passed out.

———

Water drenched my face, and I coughed and spluttered. My eyes flickered open to find Sutton looming over me, the gun in one hand and an empty bowl in the other.

"Wakey, wakey, Sienna. Can't have you passing out on me again and spoiling my fun."

I blinked, trying to clear my vision. My head felt foggy, as if my brain had been stuffed with cotton wool. I couldn't think straight.

"Max," I croaked.

"Still asleep."

I didn't know whether to be relieved he was safe or terrified that Sutton had gone to check on him and now knew where he was. I pressed a hand to my head.

"How long was I out?"

"A couple of minutes."

"Sutton, please go. I won't tell anyone you were here, I promise."

He lowered onto his haunches, those dead eyes focused directly on me. "Oh, Sienna. You always were a dumbass." He leaned in, close enough that I could smell whiskey on his breath. "Where. Is. Kathy?"

I closed my eyes and shook my head. "I don't know. Honestly. I left her in Seattle."

"Liar!"

I flinched and pressed my back into the couch, trying to put some distance between us. I thought he was going to hit me again, but then the elevator dinged, distracting him.

Dayton.

"Ah, things are about to get interesting." Sutton hauled me to my feet. He wrapped his forearm tightly around my neck, the barrel of the gun rammed against my temple once more. "Not a fucking word of warning," he murmured into my ear. "Or it's bye-bye Sienna."

I held my breath, my eyes trained on the door to the apartment, the same one Dayton would walk through at any second.

The first thing I saw was an enormous bunch of flowers. I opened my mouth to call out, but Sutton jammed the gun into the side of my head.

"Christa?"

Dayton shifted the flowers, and his eyes fell on me. He dropped the bouquet, and a few petals detached. *Dear God, don't let that be an omen.*

"What the fuck!"

"Come join the party," Sutton said, his alcohol-infused breath spattering my cheek. "All you have to do is tell me where that fucking slut Kathy Johnson is, and maybe I'll let Sienna live."

Dayton held his hands out in front of him. He never even looked at me. His eyes were fixed on Sutton, his movements slow and steady as he prowled across the wide expanse that separated the living area, where we were, from the entrance door.

"Don't do anything stupid, Atwood," Dayton said. "Right now, this is salvageable. You hurt her, and it's all over."

"I disagree," Sutton drawled. "I could kill you both, of course, but where'd be the fun in that? Nah, it'd make life much more interesting if I tied you up while I had a little fun with Sienna and forced you to watch. I mean, she's dressed for fucking, right?"

He kept the gun jammed against my temple and licked the back of my neck. I swallowed a lump of bile. My entire body shook. I couldn't breathe. My heart beat so fast, I felt as if it would explode from my body any second. His hand slipped south, and he squeezed my breast so hard it brought tears to my eyes.

"Then after I finish fucking my little whore, I could grab Max and be on a plane within the hour. By the time you'd have freed yourselves, or someone found you, there'd be a lot of miles between you and me. Good luck finding Max then." He laughed, the sound piercing my eardrums. "The thought of where he was, of what I was doing to him, would fucking kill her, slowly, torturously."

I tried to speak, but Sutton tightened his hold around my neck. I gripped his forearm and tried to burrow my fingertips between his arm and my neck to give myself some breathing space. He tightened further. Spots swam in front of my eyes. *Don't pass out. Stay with it.*

"You'd be found. Eventually," Dayton said, his voice weirdly calm. "Do you really want to live your life on the run?"

Dayton took another step, his stealthy movements barely noticeable, inching ever closer to us.

"Get. Me. Kathy."

Dayton shook his head. "I don't know where she is. If I did, I'd tell you."

"Liar!"

I flinched. Sutton hollering so close to my ear brought on a high-pitched ringing.

"I'm not lying," Dayton said.

Step.

"She means nothing to me."

Inch.

"Christa is all I care about."

Creep.

"Now put the gun down, and we can talk."

Edge.

"Don't take another fucking step!"

Dayton immediately stopped, his hands coming up in surrender mode. "Okay, easy. You're in charge."

"You've got exactly five minutes to get that fucking slut *right here* or I'm gonna put a bullet in this bitch's brain."

He jabbed me again with the barrel of the gun to press home his point.

"No!" I croaked. "Sutton, please."

Dayton's gaze shifted to me for the first time. The pain and fear in the depths of his midnight-blue eyes tore through me. They spoke volumes. *We may not survive this.*

I inclined my head. We had no choice. He'd have to get Kathy to come up here.

"Okay, okay, you win. I'll call her."

Sutton hissed, the air whistling over my cheek. "No fucking tricks, otherwise I swear, I'll fucking kill her."

Dayton's hand went to his inside pocket.

"Stop!" Sutton shouted. "What are you doing?"

Dayton froze. "My phone. It's in my pocket."

"Slowly," Sutton said. "One false move, and I'll pull the trigger."

Dayton's hand crept toward his pocket. He took out his phone and held it in the air. "See. It's cool. We're cool."

"Call her," Sutton demanded. "Do it now."

Dayton tapped the screen… and then Max's cry came over the baby monitor.

"Momma."

Sutton's head snapped to the right.

Dayton lunged.

And the gun went off.

26

DAYTON

CHRISTA SCREAMED, the noise piercing and loaded with fear. Pain exploded in my shoulder, and I fell backward. My head cracked on the floor, forcing a grunt from my throat.

I struggled to sit up, but every movement was like a thousand knives twisting in my flesh. Christa screamed again.

"Dayton!"

I forced my eyes open. She needed me. I couldn't let her down. And Max. Max was calling for her. Atwood had a gun. Fuck, my head wouldn't work. I shook it, blinking, trying to focus.

"Bastard!"

My vision cleared. Christa attempted to wrestle free of Atwood's hold, but he tightened his grip. I tried to get up, but my legs refused to obey me. Atwood had the gun pointed right at my chest. If he pulled the trigger now, I was a goner.

"Don't," I croaked, my throat painfully raw. Christ, it didn't even sound like me. I held my palm toward him as if that would save me from a bullet. "Stop."

He cocked the gun, the clicking sound sending fear rushing

through me. Not fear for me, but for what would happen to Christa, or Max, if I died.

"Fuck." I put my hand out to aid me. The floor was damp. I looked at it, covered in dark, thick, sticky blood. My blood. I felt sick, my head woozy, spinning. "Fuck," I mumbled again.

"You dick," Atwood spat. "If you'd listened and done as you were told, you wouldn't be lying there with your shoulder busted up." He kicked my phone over to me. "Now fucking. Call. Her."

"Momma!"

Max's cries urged me on. I made another attempt to get up, but my foot slipped in the blood. Pain shot through me, excruciating, lighting my shoulder on fire. My left arm hung uselessly at a very strange angle. My eyes flickered. No. Must stay awake. Dammit, brain, work. Just fucking work.

Time stood still, each second passing by as if in slow motion. I felt around for my phone, eventually closing my fingers around it. I searched for Christa. Atwood still had her in a headlock, his forearm pressing on her neck, but at least the gun was aimed at me. I willed her to look at me, and by some miracle, she did.

"Ready?" I asked.

She frowned, and then her eyes flickered to my right hand still clasped tightly around my phone. She blinked in understanding, but not before fear dashed through her eyes. With considerable effort, I managed to struggle to my feet. Blood oozed from the bullet hole in my shoulder, and nausea churned in my stomach, my head spinning from me righting myself.

"I've been ready for hours," Atwood said, completely misunderstanding that I hadn't been talking to him.

I would only have one chance to get this right. If I missed, he'd kill us both. Even if I didn't, our chances of getting out of this were slim.

Praying my days of playing baseball when I was younger didn't let me down, I took aim and threw my phone at Sutton. It caught him above his right eye, splitting the brow. He yelled and released Christa and pressed his hand to the wound. Blood seeped through his fingers. I didn't give him time to think. I launched, wrestling him to the floor. I gripped the wrist that held the gun and slammed it on the floor once, twice, three times. Pain racked through my shoulder. *Please, God, don't let me pass out.*

Atwood eventually let go, and the gun skidded away. I straddled him, fisting his hair, and bashed his head against the oak, grateful I'd never gone for carpeting.

"Let him go, Dayton."

I snapped my head to the left. Christa had hold of the gun and was aiming it right at Atwood.

"Let him go," she repeated, so calm and collected given the ordeal she'd been through. Her aim was steady, true, her arms locked, feet planted wide. Both hands were on the gun, and the barrel pointed squarely in the center of Atwood's torso.

I somehow scrambled to my feet. "Keep that trained on him. I'll call the police. I need your cell," I said, surprising myself by grinning.

"Are you okay?" she asked.

I winced as I moved. "I'll live."

She nodded then gestured at Sutton with the weapon. "Get up."

With his hand still pressed to his eye, he stood.

"Come on, baby," he said. "Let's talk."

"My cell is in the kitchen," Christa said, ignoring Atwood's plea, not that I expected her to respond.

Atwood moved.

Christa cocked the weapon. "Not another step."

I sprinted over to the kitchen, my arm hanging uselessly by my side. *I'll call Cole.* He'd be gentle with Christa, especially after the hell Atwood had put her through.

I picked her phone up off the counter, but as I went to dial, Atwood lunged at Christa. I watched, horrified, unable to get to her fast enough. The gun went off, the sound bouncing off the walls, deafening, terrifying.

"Christa!"

Atwood staggered backward, his hand now clutching his side where a red stain was fast spreading. He stumbled and fell. There was a sickening crunch when his head hit the corner of my glass coffee table.

Christa screamed. The gun fell from her hand and landed with a thud on the floor.

I sped over, patting her down, taking inventory, making sure all the pieces of her were intact. "Are you okay?" I asked, fevered. "Are you hurt?"

She looked at me, her eyes wild. "Oh God, oh God. Is he dead?"

I didn't give a shit about Atwood. "Christa! Fucking talk to me. Are you hurt?"

She shook her head. "I'm okay. I'm okay." She burst into tears.

I put my arm around her and held her. Max's cries grew over the baby monitor, but he was better staying in his room. I didn't want him to see this, and if he was crying, he was fine.

"Max."

"Leave him," I said. "We don't want him out here right now."

She nodded in understanding, then her eyes flickered to Atwood. He hadn't moved since he'd fallen, and I couldn't tell from here whether he was breathing or not. I hoped for *not*.

"I'm going to call the police, angel, okay? Then I'll call Mrs. Flannigan and get her over here to sit with Max while I get this damn bullet taken out." I grinned, trying to convey to her that I was okay.

Clearly in shock, she nodded numbly.

I rang the NYPD. It took a few moments to be patched through to Cole. Briefed, he promised to head right over.

I cut the call and crouched next to Atwood. I pressed my fingertips to his neck. Nothing. I opened one eye, and when I was met with a glassy stare, I knew he was dead.

Good.

27

CHRISTA

I HELD Dayton's hand as the ambulance sped toward the hospital. How he'd kept it together while chaos reigned, and with a bullet lodged in his shoulder, was testament to my man's grit and determination. But now we were safe, I could see the strain on his face, and the toll the blood loss had taken on him. His face had paled, and there was a sheen of sweat across his brow.

"He's going to be okay, isn't he?" I asked the paramedic, Brian, who was pushing fluids through an IV line.

"Christa, stop fussing," Dayton growled, still with it enough to call me out.

"There's your answer," Brian said. He patted my arm. "He'll be fine. The bullet didn't nick any major arteries or veins, nor from what I can tell, break any bones. You've been extremely lucky, Mr. Somers."

"Yeah, feels like it," Dayton gritted out as he grimaced through the pain.

We pulled up outside the emergency room, and Dayton was wheeled inside. After checking him over, the surgeon confirmed what I'd already feared—there wasn't an exit wound, so they'd have to operate to remove the bullet.

An hour later, he was taken to the operating room. A nurse checked me over and diagnosed a slight concussion from where Sutton had hit me with the butt of the gun, but as long as I took it easy, I'd be fine.

After filling out a bunch of forms, I made a quick call to Mrs. Flannigan to check on Max, then went to the visitors' waiting area. Cole was standing by the window nursing a drink.

"How's he doing?"

"Once they remove the bullet, the doctor said he'll make a full recovery."

"And what about you? How's the head?"

I sank into a chair. "I'm okay." I pushed my hair out of my face. "He's definitely dead, isn't he?"

Cole nodded.

I covered my face with my hands, and we sat there in silence for a few moments. I gathered my wits and took a deep breath. "Am I in trouble?"

Cole took the seat next to mine. He put his cup on the floor, between his feet. "No, you're not in trouble. We'll need a full statement from you both as soon as Dayton has recovered enough, but from my perspective, this is a clear case of accidental death. Besides, he broke into your home. You have a right to defend yourself."

I rubbed my fingertips over my dry, cracked lips. "I can't believe he's gone. I don't know whether to be relieved, or annoyed, that he'll never pay for his crimes to Kathy and Sunny. And me."

"My opinion, for what it's worth, is that the justice system is far from perfect, and perpetrators of crime sometimes get away with it. Sure, Atwood might have been facing significant prison time for the rapes if he'd been convicted, but at some point, he'd have been released. This way..." Cole shrugged. "It's over."

I nodded, my eyes filling up, and when I blinked, tears coursed down my cheeks. And once I started, I couldn't stop.

Huge, racking sobs sent my whole body into a quivering, trembling mess.

Cole rubbed my back, his touch gentle and reassuring. "It's the shock. Let it out, and you'll feel a whole lot better."

It took several minutes of uncontrolled crying before I got a hold on my emotions. Cole passed me a pack of tissues.

"Sorry," I muttered. "You don't even know me, and here I am, weeping all over you."

Cole laughed. "Believe me, I've had much worse than a pretty lady crying on my shoulder."

I smiled. I liked Detective Cole Brook. He reminded me of George in a way, with his calm demeanor and inner strength. "Can I give my statement to you?"

"Of course you can."

———

"Nina should be here soon," I said, plumping up Dayton's pillows. His left arm was in a sling, but apart from that one sign, he appeared to be in perfect health and was already itching to be released from the hospital. When I told him they wanted to keep him in for a second night, he was *not* happy. "And Detective Brook wants to talk to us."

"Is he outside?" Dayton asked.

"Yes. He came back first thing this morning."

Dayton grazed his knuckles over my cheek. "Shall we get it over with, angel?"

I nodded. "Let's."

I rose from the chair beside Dayton's bed and poked my head into the hallway. "We're ready," I said to Cole.

He came into the room with me. I perched on Dayton's bed, giving Cole the only chair. I preferred to be here anyway, closer to Dayton.

Cole systematically went through his questions. In a way, I

found it cathartic going over what had happened from the moment I'd set foot in the living room to find Sutton sitting on the couch waving that gun at me. By the time we'd finished our statements, I was exhausted.

"What happens now?" I asked.

Cole rose from the chair and tucked away his notebook. "I'll get this written up and then it'll go to my superior for signing off. Atwood's next of kin, his sister, I believe, has already been informed, so it'll be up to her to arrange the funeral."

"Did you speak to Rochelle?" I asked, nerves flooding me. I fully expected her to turn up and take out her anger and rage and grief for Sutton's death on me.

Cole shook his head. "A coworker did." He narrowed his eyes. "But if she gives you any trouble, you call me, got it?"

"We will," Dayton said.

A tap on the door interrupted us, and then it opened, and Nina entered, wheeling a suitcase behind her. Her gaze fell on Cole, and her mouth dropped open.

"I'll leave you to it," Cole said, patting Dayton's good arm. He smiled at me, then went to leave. "Ma'am," he said to Nina as he passed, then closed the door behind him.

"Wow," Nina said. "Did you see how *insanely* handsome that guy was? Those eyes." She clasped a hand to her chest. "Like, wow."

"Did you notice the thick wedding band on his left hand?" Dayton drawled. "He and his wife just had their second baby."

"Lucky girl," Nina said, pulling up a chair. "If he were mine, I wouldn't let him leave the house. I'd tie him to the bed—"

"La la la," Dayton said, sticking a finger in his ear. He'd have probably done both, but his left arm was very much out of action. "Fuck, Nina. I don't want to think about that, thank you very much."

I giggled. Nina looked unrepentant.

"I have something for you," she said, reaching into her purse.

She dropped a thick, cream envelope in Dayton's lap. "My resignation."

"What?" Dayton said, glancing at me. "Did you know about this?"

"No," I said. "I'm as surprised as you. What's going on, Nina?"

She gnawed at her bottom lip. "Orin and I want to give things a go. We've tried the long-distance thing, and it's just not working." Her lips curved into a faint smile. "I miss him, and I miss both of you, and I want to come home."

Orin Henderson, the only son of Ava and Oliver Henderson, acquaintances of Dayton's. I'd only met them once, last New Year's, but from what Dayton had told me, Nina and Orin had been involved in an on-off relationship for years. Looked as though they were finally getting serious.

"Jesus, you fickle woman," Dayton said, rolling his eyes. "Two seconds ago, you were slobbering after Detective Brook."

Nina glared. "I was not slobbering. I was merely window shopping. Did you see me get my credit card out? No. So be quiet, accept my resignation from the Chicago office, and then find me a replacement job at the New York office."

I laughed. I adored Nina and couldn't be happier that I'd get to spend more time with her when she moved back to Manhattan.

"Yes, ma'am," Dayton said. "But you're responsible for finding a replacement in Chicago."

"Dayton!" I said, glaring at him.

He shrugged, unconcerned and remorseless.

"I've already found one," Nina said. "I've been training her for weeks."

"Without my knowledge."

"Yep," Nina said, grinning. "Right under your goddamn nose."

Dayton grimaced. "As soon as I'm out of this hospital, I need to get on top of my business. I've taken my eye off the ball for long enough, and now Atwood is out of our lives, I can get back to running my company."

I suppressed a flinch at hearing Sutton's name. I wondered how long it would be before I felt truly safe. "Plenty of time for work," I said. "Let's get you fully recovered first."

"Nothing wrong with my voice," Dayton said. "I can still direct."

I arched an eyebrow. "After my surgery, you behaved like a mother hen." I winked at Nina. "It's payback time, mister."

Dayton groaned. "God help me."

"He won't help you," I said. "I've had a word with him, and he's fully on my side."

Nina chuckled. "You're screwed, brother."

Dayton smiled at me. "I guess it won't be too bad if you have to give me one or two sponge baths," he said.

"Ew," Nina said. "Same goes. I don't want to hear about your bedroom antics either, thank you very much."

Nina stuck around for a little while longer, but when the nurse arrived to check Dayton's vitals, she got up to leave.

"Shall I check into a hotel?" she asked. "Or will they have cleaned up your place by now?"

I winced, the thought of blood all over the oak flooring gave me the chills.

"I believe the police have finished, and the cleaners have been in, so you should be fine," Dayton said. "Christa, go with her." I opened my mouth to interrupt, but he cut me off. "There's no point hanging around here, and besides, you should be with Max."

I did want to see my baby. At least he'd been kept out of it, hadn't seen the horrors that had gone on at home. Mrs. Flannigan had whisked him back to her apartment and kept him overnight —God bless her. I just hoped I could continue to live in the penthouse, without imagining Sutton lying dead on my floor every time I picked up a cup off the coffee table.

I leaned over and kissed him while Nina pretended to fiddle around in her purse to give us some privacy.

"I'll be back later once Max is in bed, providing Nina doesn't mind babysitting."

Nina grinned. "I'll be happy to."

Paul put Nina's bag in the trunk and then opened the back door for us. I gestured for Nina to get in first. As I was following, a movement to my left caught my eye. I stopped and peered closer. Rochelle was getting out of a cab. Oh God, I bet she was coming to formally identify the body…

Her attention fell on me, her eyes red-rimmed where she'd clearly been crying. I couldn't help feeling a little sorry for her. Whatever I thought of Sutton, I had no doubt that she loved him and he loved her. In fact, Rochelle was the only person Sutton seemed to truly love unreservedly. She must be grieving terribly.

I held her gaze for a few moments, then climbed into the car. Rochelle was very much part of my past, and now, with Sutton gone, I had a future I could truly embrace.

28

DAYTON

"WELCOME BACK, MR. SOMERS," Angie gushed as she scooted around her desk.

For one horrifying moment, I thought she was going to try to hug me, but instead, she went for an awkward handshake. Awkward because we'd never shaken hands, not even when she'd interviewed for her job.

"Thank you. Grab your iPad and follow me. We've got lots to do."

I stepped inside my office, calm instantly settling over me. Thank God I was finally able to come back to work full time. The last two weeks cooped up in the penthouse with Christa fussing and constantly trying to shove multivitamins down my throat had given me some serious cabin fever. I wasn't the kind of man to hang around twiddling my thumbs, but every time I'd tried to knuckle down and get some work done, either Christa or Nina had appeared as if they were goddamn telepaths, removing the tablet, phone, laptop, even a pen and paper from me. Then they'd metaphorically patted me on the head like some fucking mutt and told me to get some rest.

Angie's heels clicked on my Italian tile floor, a sound that used to get on my nerves, but now, I found it oddly reassuring. Things were getting back to normal, including my legendary impatience and drive for perfection.

I sat behind my desk, Angie taking a seat opposite, iPad on her knee. I spent ten minutes rapidly barking out orders with Angie furiously tapping on her screen.

"That'll be all, Angie," I said, dismissing her. When she remained seated, I frowned. "You can go now."

She smiled at me. Angie never smiled at me, only grimaced, or frowned, or plopped out an odd tear or two when I'd been particularly demanding. "It really is good to have you back."

Oh, dear God. I managed to refrain from rolling my eyes. This new Angie was rather unsettling. I preferred the one who muttered "asshole" under her breath. I didn't know how to deal with this version.

"If you're going to get Draven here within the hour, you'd better snap to it."

I expected my sharp response to wipe the smile from her face. Instead, it grew.

"Of course, sir. I'll do that right away then fetch you a coffee and a bagel, just how you like them."

She bustled from the room, skirt swinging, heels clopping. The door closed with a quiet click, and the suppressed eye roll came. God help me. I'd have to be extra cutting with Angie for the next few days. Put her back into line.

Except, I wasn't sure I wanted to. A little over a year had passed since Christa had walked through the doors of my building and changed my life forever. A year in which so much had happened and, in the process, I'd changed. While I doubted I'd ever be described as 'soft' or 'easy-going' work-wise, it might be nice to be recognized as human by my employees from time to time.

Angie returned with my breakfast but didn't linger—thankfully. The next few hours passed by in a blur with meeting after meeting. Angie dropped off a sandwich for my lunch and bestowed another of those smiles that were starting to freak me out. I barely tasted my lunch as it went down, and although I might grumble on occasion that I didn't have time to breathe, let alone eat, in truth, *this* was what drove me, what motivated me, what validated my existence. I loved it.

"Mr. Somers, Mr. erm... Draven is here."

"Just Draven," I heard him reply, his booming voice filling my office.

Grinning, I pressed the intercom. "Send him in."

The door opened, and Draven entered. I caught a glimpse of Angie next to him, her mouth hanging open, dwarfed by the bearded, tattooed rough-around-the-edges Draven. We didn't get a lot of visitors of his ilk around here.

"Hey, good to see you," I said. "That'll be all, Angie, thank you."

She nodded and grabbed the door handle, her mouth still agape. The door snicked shut.

Draven shook my hand. I tried not to wince. He jerked his chin in my direction. "How's the bullet hole?"

I automatically stretched my shoulder. "Healing, slowly. It's a bit stiff, but as long as I continue my physical therapy, it should be good as new in no time."

"Getting shot hurts like a son of a bitch, don't it?"

"It does. I take it you've been shot, too?"

He nodded. "Twice. No more fun the second time around either."

I laughed. Draven and I were poles apart but, hell, I liked the guy. He had a wicked sense of humor and was definitely one of those people you wanted in your corner.

He took a seat opposite my desk. "How's Christa doing?"

I went around the other side and sat. "Better. She's still struggling to process it all. In her mind, she killed a man, even though the reality was very different. In my mind, I'm glad the fucker is dead."

Draven nodded. "It makes moving forward easier for both of you. Even if we'd managed to secure a conviction, he'd never have been out of your lives."

"Exactly. I refuse to feel an ounce of sympathy for him. Christa isn't quite where I am yet, despite what he put her through, both then and now." I chuckled. "She's got more heart than I have."

"And how's the little dude?"

I broke into a smile, a regular occurrence whenever I thought about Max. "Thankfully completely unaware of it all. He hasn't even asked why the man who started coming to see him a few weeks ago doesn't come around anymore. Christa and I had been prepared for questions, but they haven't come so far. Christa wants to tell him everything one day, but with any luck, we won't have to face that for a few years."

"Sweet." Draven removed an envelope out of the pocket of his leather jacket and slid it across to me. "My final bill."

I quirked a brow. "An honest to goodness invoice?"

He grinned. "What can I say? I'm legit."

I didn't even look at it as I returned his smile. Draven was anything but legit—thank goodness. If he'd played things by the letter of the law, Christa and I wouldn't have had the reassurance he'd provided whenever Max had been out of sight. "I'll arrange payment today. I can't thank you enough for everything you and your team did."

He shrugged. "I still think we let you down, though."

I narrowed my eyes. "How so?"

"Because he got inside your place."

"I never asked you to watch my home. Christa should have been safe once she was inside. It's not your fault the receptionist was a temp and fucked up."

The same receptionist who wouldn't be working in my

building ever again. The head of the condominium association had rained hell down on the agency after he'd discovered she'd been the one to allow Sutton unauthorized access. Her ineptitude could have gotten Christa killed. I didn't give a shit that she was only a temp brought in to cover sickness. Not my problem.

Draven shrugged, but I got the feeling he still felt he'd failed in some way. He was clearly a perfectionist and took his business extremely seriously. Another thing we had in common.

"Okay, well, if we're done, I'll—"

The door to my office flew open, and Christa almost fell inside. "Dayton! Oh God. It's Max. He's gone."

29

DAYTON

"WHAT DO YOU MEAN, GONE?" I asked, desperately trying not to jump to conclusions until I had all the facts.

"He's not at the childcare center." Panicked, she thrust her hands into her hair. "Sondra just called me. He's not there. She said one minute he was playing with his friends, the next he'd disappeared. I've been down there. We've searched everywhere, and he's not there!"

I briefly glanced at Draven then turned my attention back to Christa. "Okay, try to stay calm. Let's go and talk to Sondra."

"I'm coming, too." Draven said.

I nodded, grateful for his assistance. If Max had wandered off or, God forbid, been taken, then I couldn't think of anyone I'd rather be with us.

We arrived in the basement where my childcare center was housed. Sondra looked stricken, her face pale as she paced, and her lip wobbled when she spotted us. "I'm so sorry. He was there. He was right there." She pointed to the middle of the room where a few of the other kids were still playing. "We've searched everywhere, but he's definitely not here."

It wasn't that I didn't believe her, but I wanted to check for myself. Draven and I darted around the place, searching every corner, every room, including the staff restroom in case, by curiosity, he'd ended up in there. He hadn't.

I wiped my clammy palms on my jacket and, swallowing my fear, I immediately took charge. "Sondra, gather the staff together because I'm sure the police will want to talk to them. Draven, call Cole then meet Christa and me upstairs in reception. We'll be in the security room behind the reception desk."

Draven gave a curt nod and immediately made the call. I clasped Christa's hand and ran into the stairwell that led up to the lobby. I strode across to the reception desk. Wide-eyed, the receptionist stood up straight as I approached.

"Mr. Somers, what can I—"

"Nothing," I said, gesturing for her to sit back down. I marched to the door behind reception and flashed my badge over the entry pad. There was a beep, and the door opened. I grabbed a chair for Christa and sat in front of the computer screen.

I clicked the mouse, and the screen came to life. Our security system was one I was well versed in. I opened the folder for today.

"How long ago did Sondra call you?"

Christa glanced at her watch. "Fifteen minutes. Maybe twenty. Oh, please." She wrapped her arms around her body, then got to her feet and paced. "Oh God, please, don't let anything have happened to my baby."

A hard rap on the door brought my head up. "That'll be Draven. Go let him in, Christa."

She shot over to the door, and Draven joined us. "Cole will be here in a few minutes."

"Good," I said, returning my gaze to the screen.

Draven stood behind me while I pulled up the footage from the last thirty minutes. So many comings and goings went on in the lobby, but this was the only way out. If someone had taken Max, then we'd see them leave through the front entrance. And if they hadn't then he was still somewhere in this building. If that was the case, I'd order a floor-by-floor search until we found him.

I tapped on the keys while Christa fidgeted in her seat and gnawed on her fingernails. I was as scared as she was, but I had to keep it together, for both our sakes. If I panicked, that would alarm Christa even more. She needed me to hold my fear in check, to be there as a comfort and support for her, to ignore the storm brewing in my gut.

I set the recording to play at double time. Draven leaned over my shoulder, and all three of us peered at the screen, not even blinking in case we missed something. When the timer bar showed eight minutes and forty-two seconds, Christa shouted, "There!"

I paused the footage. Sure enough, there was Max, holding the hand of a woman. He was sucking on a lollypop. She had her head bent as though she was talking to him. I moved the footage on frame by frame, until her head came up.

"Oh God," Christa cried, covering her face. "Oh no, no, no."

I clenched my jaw. "Rochelle fucking Atwood."

I fast-forwarded, watching as she hesitated, scouring around, and then she slipped down the hallway between reception and the elevators.

"Where the fuck is she taking him?" I muttered.

I opened a few more files that would bring up other cameras, searching, scanning. She had to be here somewhere. It was only a matter of time before she appeared on another security tape.

"There she is," Christa and Draven exclaimed simultaneously on the fourth one I tried.

I frowned as I tried to place her location. She wasn't in what I'd call the public areas of the building. The hallway showing up on screen was of the more functional variety.

"Where is that?" Draven asked.

"I'm trying to place it."

"It's your building."

I glowered over my shoulder. "And it's fucking huge. I don't know every goddamn inch."

"Stop!" Christa cried out. "Please stop, just find him." She twisted her hands over and over. I placed mine on top of hers, stilling her.

"We'll find him," I said. "I promise you."

I tracked Rochelle to another hallway, zooming in as I spotted a door at the far end. My heart plummeted, and a shot of ice water rushed through my veins.

"Shit." I leaped to my feet. The chair I'd been sitting on tipped over with a crash. "She's on the roof."

The three of us dashed back out into the lobby. I spotted Cole getting out of a car outside and gestured to him to hurry.

"Rochelle Atwood has got Max," I hollered the second he entered. "She's on the roof."

"Then let's go."

Christa clutched my arm, her nails digging through my jacket into my skin. "Dayton, she hates me, she's insane with grief over losing Sutton, she'll want to exact her pound of flesh. Do something. Don't let her hurt my baby."

I clasped her hand and marched down the hallway, shooting her what I hoped was a reassuring smile. "She wouldn't hurt him. He's just a child. She wants attention, that's all, otherwise she'd have left the building. She wants to be found. She'll know that the first thing we'd do would be to check the security feed."

All four of us dived into the elevator. I jabbed the button, willing the doors to close faster. The car jerked as it set off.

"Now listen," Cole said, his eyes on Christa. "When we get there, you are to stay back. Hear me?"

She shook her head violently. "No. She has my baby. It's me she really wants." Her eyes filled with tears which then spilled onto her cheeks, but she didn't crumble. Far from it. Instead, she hit Cole right where it would have the most impact. "If this was your child, would you just sit back?"

He visibly winced. "No, I wouldn't."

"Then you shouldn't expect me to either."

Cole blew out a resigned breath. "Okay, but please, follow my orders. If I tell you to do something, you do it without question. Got it?"

"Yes."

The elevator stopped, and we dashed into the hallway. "Follow me," I said, turning right. At the far end was the door that led to the roof, the one we'd seen Rochelle go through with Max. I pressed down on the door handle. It didn't open.

"Fuck, she must have locked it from the other side."

"Stand back," Draven said, his gun already in his hand.

I yanked Christa away and put my arms around her. Draven shot the lock, the noise of the gun going off deafening in the narrow, closed-in hallway. He kicked the middle of the door, and it sprang open.

Cole and Draven ran forward, Christa and I right on their tails. I spotted Rochelle immediately. She had her back against the railings, Max between her legs, and she had the flat of her hand on his chest, holding him in place. A gun dangled from her right hand.

"Momma!"

"Oh God, Max."

Christa launched forward.

"Grab her," Cole called out.

I managed to catch her arm at the last second and haul her back. "Christa, wait."

She struggled in my arms, trying to free herself, to get to Max. Understandable, but as panicked as I felt on the inside, I knew we needed to play this one carefully to avoid a bloodbath.

"Let me go!" she cried. "Max. I'm here. It's okay, Momma's here."

Max wriggled, his arms out in front, wanting Christa. My chest tightened, and a burst of fury erupted within me. How *dare* this fucking bitch take my son. How *dare* she put Christa through yet more mental torture.

Rochelle's eyes were trained on Christa. She didn't waver, didn't blink, just stood completely still, but there was a wildness, an unhinged air about her. The woman had clearly tipped over the edge into insanity.

"Let's stay calm, Miss Atwood," Cole said, inching forward.

Rochelle pointed the gun at him. "Get back. Get the fuck back, or I'll kill him. I'll kill her. I'll kill every single one of you."

Cole froze. "Relax, Miss Atwood. Everything's okay. You're in charge."

"Let him go, Rochelle," I said. "You don't want to hurt Max." I couldn't believe how calm I sounded. Inside, I was a burning mess of fear and rage, but outwardly, I exuded serenity.

"Let the boy go," Cole said. "Then we can talk."

"I don't want to talk!" Rochelle screamed. She shifted the direction of the gun to Christa. "I want her to die!"

"No!" I shouted, pushing Christa behind me. "Take me. Swap me for Max."

"I don't want you. You're *nothing* to me. But she... she killed him."

Christa moved so fast, I didn't have time to grab her. She pitched forward, right into Rochelle's line of sight.

"Please, Rochelle," Christa said. "You can have me. Let Max go, and I'll stay here with you. Just us." She gestured to me, Cole, and Draven. "I'll tell them to leave. You can do whatever you want to me, but please, Max has nothing to do with this. Sutton wouldn't want any harm to come to him."

Terror for Christa's safety paralyzed me. If I tried to grab her, to pull her back to safety, Rochelle might fire the gun. I couldn't risk that, even as my instincts screamed at me to save her. I shot a helpless look at Draven.

His silent response: *Don't do anything stupid.*

Rochelle's eyes flashed with fury at the mention of her brother. She cocked the trigger. The barrel of the gun was pointed right at Christa's chest. If Rochelle fired, Christa would die. My heart pelted my ribcage. *Thud, thud, thud.* I swallowed past an obstruction in my throat. I couldn't lose her. Not now, not after everything we'd been through. *Not like this.*

"It's because of you he's dead. You killed him. He meant *everything* to me, and you took him from me."

Tension buzzed off Draven, waves of heat rolling over me. He shifted to my right, catching Rochelle's eye.

"Don't move. Any of you move, and I'll kill her."

"Easy," Draven said, his voice surprisingly soft.

Christa took a tentative step forward. "Let him go, Rochelle," she repeated. "I'm the one you want. Max is innocent. I'm the guilty one."

I sucked in a breath, keeping my focus on Rochelle, watching, waiting like a coiled spring, ready to move if I saw my chance. I didn't dare to look at Max. If I saw a hint of fear in his eyes, I'd lose it.

"Shoot me if you must, but let Max go," Christa said.

The air crackled with tension. I couldn't breathe properly. My lungs wouldn't expand to give me a good dose of oxygen.

"I know you, Rochelle," Christa continued. "You're not a bad person, and I know you'd never hurt a child on purpose. Let him go, and we can talk. You can beat me, shoot me, pull out my fingernails, slice my flesh. Whatever you want. But first, you have to release my son."

Rochelle's eyes glazed over. "I miss him," she whispered. Her breath hitched, and a single tear fell onto her cheek followed by a second and a third. "He was the only one who loved me, who cared, who knew what I needed. The only one who understood what goes on up here." She let go of Max to poke herself in the temple, but before he could move, she clamped her hand on his shoulder. "And now he's gone, what will I do? Who will help me now?"

"I'll help you," Christa said, her voice incredibly calm, although tears slowly trickled over her cheeks.

I had no idea how she was keeping it together when I was on the edge of losing my mind. Any second, this might all turn to hell, and I could lose the two people I cared for more than my own life. I was helpless, powerless to stop the nightmare unfolding in front of me.

"We were friends once," Christa said quietly. She inched closer to Rochelle. "I won't let anything happen to you."

"Liar!" Rochelle screamed.

"I'm not lying. I'll help you. Whatever you need, I'm here for you. Please, Rochelle, he's your nephew. He's innocent of any crimes. I'm the one who deserves to pay."

Rochelle's lips mashed into a thin line. "Get over here. Right here, next to me," she said through gritted teeth.

"Oh God, no," I muttered.

Christa held her hands out in front. "I'm coming. Whatever you want, Rochelle."

Christa's steps were sure as she walked to Rochelle, away from me, away from where I could keep her safe. When would this family just let her go, let her be, let her *live*? Noise roared in my ears, as loud as the sound of rushing water.

Rochelle released Max and roughly grabbed Christa's arm. I crouched and held out my arms. "Max, come here," I said, pushing authority into my voice, showing him I meant business.

"Go to Dada, Max," Christa said, a slight waver to her voice, the first sign she'd given that showed her fear.

For a split second, I thought he wasn't going to come to me, and I couldn't risk rushing forward to grab him. One false move, and Rochelle could pull the trigger.

And then he ran, right into my arms. I scooped him up, hugging him to me. His little body shook, and even though he was only three years old, he knew, he just knew he'd been part of a terrifying situation, and that it was far from over. I kissed him, then reluctantly passed him to Cole. If this ended badly—oh God, I couldn't bear it—but if it did, I would not allow Max to witness his mother's death.

"Run," I shouted at Cole. "Go, please."

Cole nodded, then left with Max. The door behind us clicked shut.

Rochelle stepped up onto the ledge that surrounded the building. "Get up here!" She hauled Christa next to her.

Oh no no no no.

I shot another desperate look at Draven. He widened his eyes and glared at me. *Stay calm.*

Christa's eyes met mine, relief that Max was safe mixed with panic that her own life could end at any minute. She mouthed, "Take care of Max."

My vision blurred. I blinked furiously. She wasn't having Christa. She wasn't taking my girl with her on her trip to Hell. I needed to switch tactics, and fast. I had to—somehow—find a way of reaching Rochelle, of getting her to trust me.

"Thank you for letting Max go, Rochelle," I said, the merest trace of a quiver to my voice. "I know this is hard. I know you're suffering. You loved your brother, I get it. I have a sister, and I adore her. I couldn't bear it if anything happened to her. But you have to believe me when I say that Sutton's death was an accident. Christa didn't kill him. There was a struggle, and the gun went off."

"No," she bit out, her nostrils flaring. "No, she killed him."

She roughly yanked on Christa's arm. Christa's eyes flared.

Fear clogged my throat. They were so close to the damn edge. Too close. Adrenaline flooded my system, pumping through my veins. I took a few shallow breaths, keeping my body still.

"You don't want to do this, Rochelle," I said. "I can help you. Whatever you need, it's yours. You can trust me. I'm just like Sutton." Even saying that fucker's name knocked me sick. We were nothing alike, but I'd say anything, *do anything* to save Christa. "If he were here, he'd make it all better, wouldn't he? He'd fix things for you. Let me be that person. Let me help you."

Rochelle's tears flowed, and she hitched a sob, gulped, then shook her head violently. "It's too late," she whispered, so quietly her words were swept away on the breeze. "I don't want to live without him. I won't make it without him."

She shifted her body weight, glanced briefly over her shoulder. Her hand tightened on Christa's arm.

Oh fuck, no.

Draven and I simultaneously sprang forward.

Rochelle toppled backward.

I grabbed Christa, dragging her off the ledge. We fell to the ground. She grunted as she landed on top of me.

"Jesus, fuck, are you okay?" My arms went around her. She didn't utter a word. "Talk to me!" I shouted. "Tell me you're okay."

She finally nodded. Her hands fisted in my shirt, and black mascara streaked down her cheeks as her tears fell. Her entire body trembled violently, and she buried her face in my neck.

Draven peered over the side of the building then turned to us, a grim expression tugging his mouth down. "I'll get Cole to call it in."

He left us alone on the roof. Anger flooded through me. I gripped her face, staring her right in the eyes, my hands shaking as I held her. "Don't you ever fucking do that again. Don't you ever fucking do that to me again. Jesus… fuck…" I hugged her tightly to me. "You scared the shit out of me. I thought I'd lost you. God…"

"I'm sorry, I'm so sorry," she sobbed. "Oh God, Max. Please take me to Max. I need to hold my baby."

I helped her to her feet, but when her knees buckled, I virtually had to carry her off the roof. Cole and Draven were standing about halfway down the hall. Cole was on the phone, Max settled on his hip. Christa tore out of my arms and ran to Max, scooping him into her arms. She covered his face in kisses while he clung to her, his tiny fists gripping her sweater.

"Oh, baby." She buried her nose in his hair, smelling him, kissing him over and over. "I love you baby. I love you so much."

I went to join my family, wrapping them in my arms. It was over. It was finally over.

30

CHRISTA

One year later

I DROPPED my sunglasses back into place and smiled as I watched Dayton and Max splash around in the ocean. We'd been really lucky with the weather this weekend. It wouldn't be long now before the leaves began to fall, and the warmth of the late summer sunshine would give way to clouds, and rain, and eventually snow.

I did love it at the Cape, though. Dayton had suggested flying to Europe, to the Mediterranean, but I hadn't felt up to traveling that kind of distance, especially when I was this far along.

Right on cue, my daughter kicked as if to say "Don't blame me." I rubbed my belly, my scars barely visible now, and hummed a tune that always seemed to settle her when she became particularly active. Three months until I got to meet her, and I couldn't wait.

I pulled up my knees and rested the small, leather-bound journal against them. I opened it and began to read.

"I thought you weren't going to look at those anymore."

I lifted my head and squinted up at Dayton. "I wasn't, but I can't seem to stop myself."

He sat on the edge of my sunbed, his eyes briefly flickering to Max, who was digging in the sand a short distance away.

"I really wish you wouldn't. What good can it do?"

I shrugged, glancing down at Rochelle's journal once more. The police had found a stack of them when they'd searched the apartment she'd been renting in New York. Once they'd finished their inquiries into her death, I asked if I could have them. As no one came forward to claim her personal effects, they said I could. Dayton didn't understand why I wanted to read her private thoughts. I wasn't sure I understood either.

"I guess I'm searching for answers that I know I won't get. Closure maybe."

He reached out a hand to stroke my belly. I closed my eyes and reveled in the bliss of his touch.

"She's kicking," he said, wonder and awe prevalent in his tone.

"Yeah, she's doing a lot of that at the moment. Keeps me up half the night."

"Well, if you get bored, I may have some ideas to keep you entertained." He leaned across and planted a kiss right in the center of my bump.

I chuckled. "I'll bear that in mind." I closed the journal and set it on the sand. "Poor Rochelle. I feel kind of sorry for her. She had such a sad life. Another woman manipulated by Sutton. Her life was so tied to his that without him, she had nothing. She didn't know how to exist after he'd gone."

He glared at me. "She almost killed you. She could have killed Max. She was batshit fucking crazy."

I shook my head. "She was sick. She must have been mentally ill to do what she did. I honestly don't think she was evil, Dayton, just misguided and manipulated by Sutton. She turned on me because *he* turned on me. She was his puppet, without a mind of her own. She had no clue who she was deep down, and so when he died, she became rudderless."

He drew my hand to his lips and kissed my palm. "Your empathy is wasted on her, but it's another sign of just what an amazing woman you are. But you need closure. We both do. I think the best thing to do would be to burn these journals." He caressed my belly once more. "It's time to move on. To truly put the past behind you. We have so much to look forward to."

My gaze drifted to Max, then back to Dayton, his expression pleading. I knew he was right. And maybe by destroying the journals, Rochelle would find her peace in death.

"Okay. Let's burn them."

———

I cleared away our dinner things, and Dayton put Max to bed. The stack of Rochelle's journals sat on top of the dining table—all ten of them. She'd certainly been prolific, her ramblings starting at the age of sixteen, long before I'd ever met her. From what I'd discovered, writing was her way of trying, desperately, to find herself, yet all the while being controlled by Sutton, making self-discovery impossible.

Thankfully, Max hadn't been traumatized by his experience on top of Dayton's building. For weeks afterward, I'd waited for the nightmares to start, but apart from the first week or two when he'd been more clingy than usual, he'd soon returned to his normal, happy-go-lucky self.

George had informed us that following Sutton's death, another four women had come forward to report that he'd raped and beaten them, too. That made six women, plus me, who he'd violated—and for all we knew there could be more. It was a terrible club to belong to. The only good thing to come of it all was that I'd made a new friend in Kathy. She'd remained in New

York after Sutton's death, and Dayton, true to his word, had allowed her to stay living in the apartment and hired her into his company.

I heard Dayton coming down the stairs and greeted him with a smile. He held out his arms, and I went willingly. I couldn't snuggle as close to him these days with Miss Bump taking up so much space, but I managed pretty well. He tipped up my chin and brushed my lips softly.

"Shall we?"

I nodded. Dayton picked up six of the books, I grabbed the other four, and we went outside. He'd already set up a garbage can in the back yard. I had no idea where he'd sourced it from, but I didn't bother asking. It didn't really matter, and I was used to things magically appearing where Dayton was concerned.

He dropped his six volumes inside, and I did the same with mine. Squirting a little lighter fluid on top of them, he instructed me to stand back. Then he lit a match and tossed it into the barrel. Flames instantly took hold. We stood a safe distance away and watched Rochelle's life's work burn. By the time the books had been turned to ash, a sense of peace had settled over me.

"You were right," I admitted. "Burning them has given me closure."

He settled an arm around my shoulder. "I'm sure we've had this conversation before. I'm always right."

I cocked an eyebrow. "You wish."

He laughed and hugged me to him. We stood for a while, watching the orange glow from the fire wither and die, allowing us to see the stars twinkle in the night sky. I shivered as the temperature dropped, and Dayton insisted we go back inside the house.

"Want a drink to take up to bed?" I asked.

He snagged me around my non-existent waist. "No, I just want to take you to bed." His mouth covered mine, and he traced my bottom lip with his tongue before starting a dance that I knew so well but could never get enough of.

The dance that was ours and ours alone.

The dance of our love.

* * *

If you enjoyed this duet, then why not check out my new series, Full Velocity. The first book, Friction, releases August 2019.

Hot, super-rich racing drivers - check.
Feisty women who'll bring them to their knees - check
Every book a standalone with guaranteed HEA - double check.
Order your copy today!

Or maybe you're in the mood for a good ugly cry. We all need one of those occasionally to blow away the cobwebs. Grab your copy of My Gift To You right now.

FROM ME TO YOU

Thank you so much for reading Avenging Christa.

I've loved the experience of writing with another author. It's definitely something I'd like to explore more in the future.

Mel Comley is simply one of the most generous people I know, both with her time and her advice. I value her friendship enormously.

I really hope Avenging Christa gave you the satisfying ending you were hoping for. Sutton Atwood is one of the vilest characters I've ever had inside my head. At times it was a pretty uncomfortable place to be. I can't help feeling a twinge of sadness for Rochelle though. I wonder what her life would have been like if she'd had a different family?

<u>Like an author - leave a review.</u>

Reviews really help readers discover new books, as well as putting a great big smile on my face!

You can share your thoughts on Amazon, Goodreads, or on Bookbub, or feel free to contact me directly.

Why not follow me on Amazon to be alerted when I have a new release out. Alternatively, you can also follow me on Bookbub and those kind folks will also let you know there's a new book for you to discover.

FRICTION - BLURB

Jared Kane...

Our new racing driver.
God on the track.
And the man I didn't know I wanted until I fell into his arms and
kissed him before uttering a single word.
He's resisting me at every turn.
But he's wasting his time.
I always get what I want.
And I want Jared Kane.

Paisley Nash...

The boss's daughter.
Spoiled, entitled, tenacious, and spunky.
She's completely off limits—until I'm warned not to touch her.
Then it's game on.
Except taking her to my bed might cost me everything I've
fought hard for.
No woman is worth that.
Not even Paisley Nash

BOOKS BY TRACIE DELANEY

The Winning Ace Series

Cash - A Winning Ace Short Story

Winning Ace

Losing Game

Grand Slam

Winning Ace Boxset

Mismatch

Break Point - A Winning Ace Novella

Stand-alone

My Gift To You

The Brook Brothers Series

The Blame Game

Against All Odds

His To Protect

Web of Lies

Irresistibly Mine Series

Tempting Christa

Avenging Christa

Full Velocity Series

Gridlock

Inside Track (coming soon)

.

ACKNOWLEDGMENTS

Sometimes when I'm writing my thanks to my amazing team, it feels a little bit like a broken record. But really, they're so amazing that all I can do is wax lyrical about how lucky I am to have these terrific people as part of my team.

To hubs… thank you for putting up with me each and every day. For your patience when I go into myself because I'm talking to my characters instead of you! I couldn't do this without your unwavering support. You're my world.

To Mel… well, it's over. (Crying emoji). I adored working on this duet with you. We should definitely look at hooking up sometime in the future. Who knows, maybe one day I'll dip my toe into the thriller/crime genre. Sutton Atwood certainly gave me a good grounding! Evil bastard LOL.

To my critique partner, Incy—once again, my gratitude seems so paltry in comparison to the generosity you shower on me each and ever day. Thank you, thank you, thank you, from the bottom of my heart.

To Louise. Mon Capitan. I love and appreciate you so very much. Thank you for everything you do.

To Del - Foxy. Once again, your work on this book was outstanding. Those little comments that send my thought process in a different direction are invaluable. I hope we work together on many more projects in the future.

To my alpha reader, Allison. Your support for this series has been invaluable. I don't have the words to express my gratitude.

To my ARC readers. You guys are amazing! You're my final eyes and ears before my baby is released into the world and I appreciate each and every one of you for giving up your time to read—and point out the odd errors that slip through the net!

And last but most certainly not least, to you, the readers. Thank you for being on this journey with me. It still humbles me to think that my words are being read all over the world.

If you have any time to spare, I'd be ever so grateful if you'd leave a short review on Amazon or Goodreads. Reviews not only help readers discover new books, but they also help authors reach new readers. You'd be doing a massive favor for this wonderful bookish community we're all a part of.

ABOUT TRACIE DELANEY

Tracie Delaney realized she was destined to write when, at aged five, she crafted little notes to her parents, each one finished with "The End."

Tracie loves to write steamy contemporary romance books that center around hot men, strong women, and then watch with glee as they battle through real life problems. Of course, there's always a perfect Happy Ever After ending (eventually).

When she isn't writing or sitting around with her head stuck in a book, she can often be found watching The Walking Dead, Game of Thrones or any tennis match involving Roger Federer. Coffee is a regular savior.

You can find Tracie on Facebook, Twitter and Instagram, or, for the latest news, exclusive excerpts and competitions, why not join her reader group.

Tracie currently resides in the North West of England with her amazingly supportive husband and her two crazy Westie puppies, Cooper and Murphy.

Tracie loves to hear from readers. She can be contacted through the following platforms

www.traciedelaneyauthor.com

traciedelaneyauthor@gmail.com

https://www.bookbub.com/authors/tracie-delaney

ABOUT M.A. COMLEY

M. A. Comley is a New York Times and USA Today bestselling author of crime fiction. To date (April 2019) she has over 90 titles published.

Her books have reached the top of the charts on all platforms in ebook format, Top 20 on Amazon, Top 5 on iTunes, number 2 on Barnes and Noble and Top 5 on KOBO. She has sold over two and a half million copies worldwide.

In her spare time, she doesn't tend to get much, she enjoys spending time walking her dog in rural Herefordshire, UK. Her love of reading and specifically the devious minds of killers is what led her to pen her first book in the genre she adores.

Look out for more books coming in the future in the cozy mystery genre.

Facebook.com/Mel-Comley-264745836884860
Twitter.com/Melcom1

Bookbub.com/authors/m-a-comley
https://melcomley.blogspot.com

26348786R00139

Printed in Great Britain
by Amazon